You, Man, Emotion

Jonathan Swerdlow

Expansions Publishing Company, Inc.

Copyright © 2023 Jonathan Swerdlow

All rights reserved.

Published by:

Expansions Publishing Company, Inc.
P.O. Box 12
Saint Joseph, Michigan 49085 USA
www.expansions.com

ISBN: 979-8-9871197-0-9

www.jonathanswerdlow.com

Dedication

To those with warm hearts in a cold place who know
who they are

Dedication

To those with warm hearts in a cold place who know who they are

Contents

Introduction

Today's world is not very human. But we are humans all the same. Our thoughts, our dreams, our aspirations. Everything that we feel. That is what makes us human. And we really aren't all so different.

We have different experiences. Different thoughts. Different dreams. Different aspirations. I would be cautious, though, to say that we have different feelings. It is our emotions that make us human – who we are is unique; what we are is the same.

The purpose of this collection is to explore that idea: that through different people in different situations, I might share with you certain feelings. Perhaps not my own feelings. Perhaps not those of others. But feelings nonetheless. My goal is to explore what it means to be human. Especially in a not-so-human world.

While the included pieces are often influenced by my own experiences or those of people I know, their purpose is for you to see yourself. To engage in self-reflection. To see yourself in others. To understand yourself and others. I can't claim that this collection is quite so profound. But I can try. And I would ask of you the same.

I sit here now upon a stone
My one and solid ground
That when I speak, it resonates
Speaking back in likened tone

From my seat I see the world:
The lives that run below,
The clouds above in full,
And its heart that has run cold

"Stone of mine, what do you think
Of all of those beneath our feet
Thinking life will never wreak
The thought of which makes my heart sink"

Echoes of my words rang forth
Reaching deep within my seat
Answers coming in swift return
Ringing off the broken earth

"Though these men are but naïve,
No solid ground on which to stand,
Thinking all shall go as planned,
Only happiness shall such thoughts leave"

So I sat and simply wondered
Though my perspective is on high,
My seat is cold and lonely
Could this be what I have blundered

"Stone of mine, are you not weak
You stand so bold and strong
With confidence, you're never wrong
But you lack a heart from which to speak"

Off the rocks, my words bounced
Turning clouds to gentle rain,
The wind to gentle force,
Tolling answers to be announced

"Though I have no heart to feel,
This is not your world—
That which happens beneath our feet
Are the only things truly real

"The rain drops wear me thin,
The wind blows me away,
But such is the course of life—
As what exists beneath your skin

"For I am free to play my part
And know that I belong
For what I am is who I am
Even if I have no heart

"Though you lost your innocence
To see the world on high,
The place you fit is down below
You must embrace it for its immanence"

So I got up from the stone
And saw the cost of my presence:
The many pits my tears had worn
As I ventured off to life unknown

Ocean Red

I'm drifting through an ocean. Up above, the sky is blue. The air is calm; the sun is warm; the water cool. Waves crash up against me. Nothing I can't stop. There hasn't been a storm for as long as I've been drifting.

No boats in sight. No land in sight. Not a speck against the shining water. No fish disturb me. No birds overhead. No craft above. Only the occasional visit of the moon so far away.

The nights are calm and peaceful. I'm carried on a sea of stars. The sound of gentle lapping guides me to the day. Clouds come by on occasion, blocking out the sun. The cracks between them shine with light, reaching tendrils from the sky gently reaching beneath the ocean.

I lost track of time. I lost track of myself. One with the waves, I go where I am taken. How long it has been, I do not know. Nor where I was or where I am. All I am is drifting.

My mind is empty. I have no thoughts. I have become the ocean. The salty air. The ripples around me. The rise and fall of time. The reflection of the sky. It is me. I am it. I no longer know the difference.

But I am hungry. I am thirsty. My flesh is raw and cracked. This ocean is so great and vast, reaching off in every direction. And there's nothing here. A sea of red. I drift upon every drop I've bled.

I am the ocean. The ocean is me. There is nothing beneath but the blood from my veins. Rising, falling, with the tide, circling the earth. There's nothing left. Nothing at all. Nothing left to be or feel.

The calm above. Its contrast below. Red on blue until the night. The night is calm. But I am not. I dream that I am sailing. That land remains to visit – islands of each and every type. One by one, I explore. Places from my past. The people I abandoned. Faces that I wished to know. The dreams that I lost hope. The future that couldn't be.

First was my past, my childhood home. By the shore, it sat on a paved island just big enough for a neighborhood. In the windows, I saw all my friends and family. They gathered in my house, all happily chatting

8

along. So I disembarked and stepped inside. Their faces grew unfamiliar. They looked at me with fear in their eyes, calling out: "Who is this stranger?"

"It is me!" I said. I named them one by one. I told them of our stories, the bonds that we did grow. But they looked at me with fury: "What does this stranger think he knows?" I begged and pleaded, but what hope did I have? For me, they had no love.

They surrounded me, holding one another. Watching me like a vicious animal. "Get out!" they yelled. "But it's me!" I whimpered. "You have no face we've ever known," they said, grabbing me, pushing me, forcing me outside.

I returned to my ship, watching familiar faces in the windows. Now that I was gone, their joyous gathering resumed. I sighed in exasperation, looking down into the ocean. In that sea of red was not a face, rather an emotion. Blood streaming from the eyes. A terrible, twisted form. This is what I've become. Thus was born my ocean.

Next came the jungle, a tower of leaves on the horizon. I was greeted by a sandy beach. Black sand covering sun-bleached skulls. I made my way into the trees.

Their bark morphed as I walked. Shifting patterns making shapes. The leaves above rustled, sending whispers to my ears. "You never asked me," was the first voice I heard. I quickly spun around.

There was a face that I let go. Part of the past that always haunts me. "I never had the chance," I pleaded. The branches bent. The bark twisted. A looming figure in the tree. Bending down. Face before me. Voice crackling like the twigs: "But you never tried." In the bark, I saw disgust. In my heart, I felt my broken trust. Tears fell, thickened sap, as the tree bent back into position, leaving a trail of red. I stared in shock.

I walked away, unable to think. Then I heard the faintest whisper, dry and weak: "Why did you do it?" A leaf brushed my neck. There, behind me, was a face whose sight brought tears to my eyes. "I felt the same," I begged, "I really tried." Branches bent upon themselves. Leaves wove like fabric. Before me stood an image captured in a tree: "You tried?" it spat. "You tried your best to break me."

And I cried. And I collapsed. Crushed by the weight of guilt. That the only thing for which I wished should curse my name before me: "I didn't have a choice. It wasn't my fault. Life was cruel instead!"

Fingers reached, verdant tendrils, lifting up my chin: "Next time think of others before you invite them to your life. Now look at what you've done." And the perfect image fell apart. Not even here could I say goodbye before the leaves turned red and crumbled.

The trees around me grew distant faces. Whispers turned to screaming, shouting what I did. The things I never did. The consequences they had. I could take no more. So I returned to the shore.

Then it was a planet, floating in the sky. An impossible feat, it hovered above, drawing up the ocean. A bridge was formed. My ship was pulled. I landed outside a city.

Come ashore, I was greeted. Robots looking like people. "Newcomer," they said, "welcome to our home. Let us bid you welcome." They told me to follow, that they would show me around. They told me that all visitors take joy in their world. My heart was lifted at the thought: a respite from the red; to see something beautiful, anything that wasn't dead.

They took me to a plaza. A dancing sculpture stood before me. Such shapes as I had never known. Shifting, morphing, with elegant form. Though ever so oddly familiar. "This is our creator's greatest work of art," they said, "proudly featured here for all to see." I watched it move, a living work. It stirred something deep inside. Why did it seem familiar?

We ventured off into a gallery. Pictures and paintings unlike anything else. "These are glimpses of other worlds – from which our creator draws inspiration," they said. I stared in awe, each perfect piece. Not a single flaw to be found. How I once dreamt of other worlds. How I once longed to visit. To see them here, so alive and real, filled me with a homesickness ever so bitter sweet.

And off they took me to see this man. "Our creator knows each and every person. Everyone in this land he calls a friend. He dreamt of a world where humans are human. And we are part of this plan."

Leaving the coast, we traveled through fields. Vibrant greens and sweeping towers. Groups of children ran all around, a robot always in tow. All around were smiling people, greeting one another with hugs, waving as we passed.

And those distant towers, so pearly white. Terraces draped in greenery. "What are they?" I asked my companions.

"Those are where the humans live," they said proudly, "where food is grown, events are held, and everything else that makes them human. Our creator says people just need to belong, and having a purpose is what makes them bond."

After some time I didn't feel pass, we arrived at a house atop a mountain, overlooking the world below – the air filled with birdsong. The door opened to reveal an old and gentle man. "Hello, newcomer," he greeted me warmly, gesturing me into his home. But I didn't move. Everything I had seen was all too familiar. I looked at his face and knew what I saw: behind the wrinkles, that face was mine.

"Who are you?" I asked. He stood, unmoving. "Who is he?" I asked, looking to the robots. But they were not there. I looked back at the lands we had passed. But there was nothing to be seen. All I saw was an ocean of red. Hands reaching from beneath. People grasping pearly white debris. Cries for help filled the air. "What is going on?" I asked, turning back. But the man was lying on the ground. I knelt beside him, and heard him rasp: "What did you do to my world?" Tears slid down his face.

"I've done nothing! I only just arrived," I said. He rasped and wheezed and looked at me. He said with one last breath: "How quickly, then, you've killed my dreams."

His home became an island. There, I was stranded. Until I saw my ship, slowly closing in. It drifted with the tide – sailing on my ocean red.

Finally, I came across a small cottage. There was room for little else. A weeping willow tree, a stone picnic table, the tiniest of gardens. My ship had more room.

When I reached the land, the door flung open. Out came two children, a boy and a girl. "Father is home!" they cheered. They ran over and hugged me. At first I didn't know what to do. Then I heard a voice: "Well, are you coming in?" She stood there in the doorway. A haunting memory. A vision I'd seen before. I called her name. She looked at me. The children grabbed my hands and brought me over. "You look terrible," she said, "but at least you're just in time for dinner."

The children brought me to a small table. "How was your trip?" asked the boy. "My trip?" I asked. "Your trip," called the woman, she caught my eye. "Are you alright?" she asked, growing a frown.

"Yes," I told them, what else could I say, "maybe just disoriented."

"Disoriented?" she replied. "From what?"

The children's faces shared her concern. I looked at them, taking them in. Do I tell them the truth? That I don't know who I am? Do I lie to them? And try to belong?

"Did it go well?" asked the girl. I didn't know what else to say, so I said "I don't know." They all gave me a look like I was playing a game. "Are you sure you're alright?" asked the woman, sounding worried.

Unsure of what else to do, all I could say was "Yes." The woman came with plates of food. "Why don't you two go downstairs," she told the children. Without a sound, they were gone. She sat beside me, uncomfortably close. She put her hand on my back. I was paralyzed with fear. Who is this woman that takes a face I know? Why do these people think of me as family?

"You don't need to talk now," she said. I felt her compassion. "But we're having guests tomorrow. I could tell them you're still resting."

"Yes," I said, "that would be best. In fact, I think I'll head to bed."

"Alright," was all she said. So I got up, eyes darting all around. Where is my bed? I saw the cottage from outside. There wasn't much room. If the children went down, then we must share a basement. All I saw was a hatch. There must be a ladder. I didn't see the children go, but where else could it be? I lifted the hatch, the woman watching me, her look of concern. There was a ladder. I climbed down.

"Captain!" yelled a voice from behind. Was I a captain? Was this tomorrow's guest, here, already? My eyes were yet to adjust. A dim red light filled the room. "Captain!" it came again. I looked over. There was a man, urgently motioning me. I ran over, lost and confused. "What are you doing? They need you in the control room!"

I entered the door beside him. The room was filled with people wearing elaborate uniforms. Lights were flashing. Sirens wailed. The only empty seat was high in the middle. But this was not a basement. Nor a boat.

They all looked at me, expectantly, glancing at the chair. I walked over. I didn't recognize the controls. "Captain!" they called. I didn't know what to do. "Get us out of here!" they called. There was no way to hide. So I just told them: "I don't know what to do."

They looked at me, dejected. Though not a look of blame. "So this is the end?" asked the man from before. He had come up beside me. "End of what?" I asked. He looked at me, that same look of concern: "The end."

Everyone grimaced. The room rattled. More lights began flashing. Sirens grew louder. "Any minute now," he said. A voice called from across the room: "Thank you for trying, sir." For trying what? I wanted to ask, but enough was enough.

I heard a crash, then instantly silence. The room fell dark, and I could see nothing. Then I felt the sun. I opened my eyes. There was the woman, her daughter and son. Lifeless. On the shore. Beneath the ruins of my ship. The cottage, now gone. The island, no more. All lost to the ocean red.

Did I do this? My ship? This innocent family? I ran to the rubble, searching for the hatch. I dug through the stones until I saw it. I ripped it off and hurried down. But all I saw were beds, two small, one large. I climbed back out and sat in despair. How did I get here? This wasn't my plan... but they were my dreams. To know someone. To be someone. To be someone known.

Then the sun rises. And I am alone. Without even myself.

What have I done? To drift upon all this emotion? Where did these people go? Where have I gone? My only rest is torment. Such is my ocean. My ocean. I created this.

Is it too late now? To live differently? Now that I have seen the truth? I would talk to all the people. Tell them how I feel. I would think about their feelings, and how I make them feel. I would try to be myself. To not get lost in dreams. And what dreams I have, I would do my best to make real. I would try. And I would try. If only I had a chance to try.

Home Above, Home Below

My home is there, up in the stars. How my heart yearns for the night that I might look to the sky. That somewhere there, so very far away, is a place that I call mine – the home I long to stay.

But I've been cast aside. I've long been forgotten. My people left me here, they didn't leave me a choice. They said they'd return, but they never did. Now I'm just an alien, trying to fit in.

"Be normal," they said, "you look just like them."

"What is normal?" I asked. "I don't know what they are."

"They're humans," they said, "they'll take you right in."

With that, they were gone. I didn't think it was so bad. A great adventure to be had, making a home in this land. Earth, they said, was a beautiful place. And they weren't wrong, it makes my home look like a disgrace. Though each has their charm, I shouldn't be unkind. But all of these mountains and valleys and rivers and lakes – everything my eye sees fits perfectly in its place.

"What beauty there is," I told my people back home, "I'm glad you sent me. I can't wait to teach these people how to be happy."

"How good to hear," they signaled back, "we'll be around next year to bring you back."

I was happy and free, the world was my work. Another broken people, nothing I hadn't seen before. But my joy was soon foiled when my communicator broke.

"Can you hear me?" I asked. There was no reply.

"Are you there?" I would say, but nobody answered.

"Will you be here next year," my voice trembled with fear.

"Is anybody out there?" They were giving me a scare.

Nothing but silence, I didn't know what to do. The only thing I could was to go and get started. So I followed the plan and made myself at home. Surrounded by mountains where I could see the stars. I chose the perfect country, a place where people didn't have so many scars.

When I first arrived, I was quick to get settled. The first thing to do was get myself work. Then I could meet people, begin the next step. I could show them what it means for them to be human. Though first it was me who had to learn and understand.

I started by watching their movies and shows. I read their books and listened to their music. Everything I experienced quickly made me sick. Is this what it means, this human race? That everyone around me is hiding their face? I am the alien, but I wear no disguise. But these people that surround me, what have they to hide?

I wondered if that was the nature of their art, whether only the darkest, most damaged of minds would think up such songs with such sorrowful rhymes; that surely not everyone goes proclaiming they're fine. These were the people who needed my help. My only hope was that these were an uncommon kind.

At last I went out and started my job. I worked reception at a regular hotel. It was a good place to listen to the stories people tell. But all that I heard were songs of caged birds. Tales of people who weren't so well. They told their stories, but not with their words. As hard as I tried, I could get no one to confide.

"How are you?" I would ask, watching their faces.

"I'm fine," they answered, without any contemplation.

"That's not so good," I told them at first.

"I'm sorry?" they would say, I could see their confusion.

"You're telling me you're fine without giving it a thought, but unless you say you're well, I would guess this is only what you've been taught."

Often, they would laugh, give me a pat on the back. They would say I was funny, joke I was strange. A few would get angry, but nothing ever changed. I worked the job for only a month. The only human I knew was my colleague at lunch. A friend I had made because we sat alone.

"You're leaving already?" he asked me sadly.

"I don't have a choice," I tried to explain, "the people I meet won't show me their pain."

"Is that why you always joke with the guests?"

"It isn't a joke. I thought you, of all people, had guessed."

He paused for a minute, looking off in the distance.

"But why do you ask them? You wouldn't share your struggles with a stranger."

"Why not?" I asked, hoping my identity wasn't in danger.

"Would you tell just anyone the problems you have going on?"

"I would," I said, "if somebody asked."

He thought again. The minutes passed. Our break was already over. I got up. He looked at me, with a smile to my surprise.

22

"Let's meet again some time," he said with life in his eyes.

And we did. Time and time again. He taught me much. He shared his story. He showed me how to be human.

"What about you? What's your story?" he finally asked.

He tried before, but I avoided the question. It had been four months. The thought of my family filled me with emotion. But of all people, he deserved to know.

"I lost contact with my people. They sent me here on a mission. They said the earth is broken, and I must spread an idea. But now that I've lost contact, I don't know how to feel."

"That's an unusual story," he said. "Your words are always so strange. But I think I know what you're saying – you and your family are estranged?"

"That's one way to put it," I replied. "Now I don't know if I have any purpose. I'm trying to be human, but I still don't even know what that is."

"So why did they send you? Did they do it for the money?"

"I wish I could send some. I'm sure they'd find it rather funny. But I just came to learn, to see what is broken."

"Do you always talk in riddles? If I didn't know any better, I'd say you're an alien."

"And if I knew no better, I'd say I really am."

23

We laughed at that, though for different reasons. But were we really so different, me and this man?

More months went by. It was harder than I thought. I still longed for the sky, but I was feeling at home. Nine months, I'd been trapped, and only one human had I known. But that was all it took – what made this place home – all of the beauty that he had shown.

I had worked four jobs. Though none of them worked. I tried to make friends, but they stuck with their friends. And outside of work, nobody wanted to talk. Though they seemed so alone, they would rather just walk.

My friend had told me why this was. He said everyone was lonely, and they carried such pain. He said life is a game, but there aren't any winners. Everyone is trying to make it through the day so they can return to their homes and make use of their pay. Nobody cared what anyone else had to say. Their only friends were the children with whom they used to play.

I asked him why that was and what about himself. He said he had friends from his past, but the bonds they once shared did not last. They shut themselves away, working all the time. They still found time for fun, but only when they could. Because life was a game, and they wanted to win. So they did what they should no matter the cost – there was plenty of time, but none to be lost.

"Then what can I do, if I don't have anyone? If I want to be human, don't I need a place where I belong?"

"Maybe that's the problem, we're not human anymore. We don't struggle to survive, so now life is a chore. Maybe we'd be better off without our emotions. At least if we didn't feel, then life wouldn't be such a bore."

"But you're not bored of living, I know that isn't you." Hearing him say that had made my heart sore.

"No, I'm not, but I'm also not living. I dream of nature, spending my days outside. I want people there with me without pain to hide. So we can be happy, together, and free. We can build houses and live like family. It's not that I can't do this because of technology. I think that's what most people would blame for what they see. But I think we took our humanity and took out the human – and this we call society."

I saw him, then, after nine whole months. For the first time, I understood. What it means to be human. I'd given up on my plan – without my people, what could I do? And this is exactly what all humans knew.

The Forest of Shadows

I entered the Forest of Shadows. Trees loomed everywhere I looked. Everything cast eerie, unnatural shadows, making the forest feel like it was closing in around me. In only a few steps, I could not even make out the way I entered.

The drive hadn't been that long, but the sun seemed to fear this place. As soon as I stepped past the first tree, it had set. Maybe I lost track of time. I left just before dawn, after all. But the closer I got, the faster darkness set in.

I held out my hand. I stared in awe at its shadow on the ground. There was hardly any light. The moon was not out. Treetops clustered overhead. Yet everything cast a shadow. I quickly realized why people fear this place. Something wasn't right.

The locals treat it like a graveyard. They say the dilapidated cars at the forest boundary are gravestones – nobody leaves the Forest of Shadows. Of course, this is just what people say. They also say there is a lake somewhere in the middle. How can they say there is a lake if nobody ever leaves? In any case, I came for the lake: the Lake of Souls in the Forest of Shadows – how poetic. The story goes that on clear nights, it reflects the souls of the lost. The only way to find the lake is to follow the calls of these lost souls from the trees. They say that if you enter the water, you become a part of the forest.

Even though I don't believe the stories, I wanted to see the Lake of Souls for myself. I've always wondered whether there was anything more to life. It would be nice to know that we have a soul. And if the stories turn out to be true, that's a risk I'd gladly take. At this point, that's all I care about. I didn't plan to leave.

Deeper and deeper I went. The forest grew darker and darker. I could barely see the trees in front of me. Once again, I held out my hand. And on the ground was its shadow. Even against the darkness, it was crisp and clear. I stood and admired it for a minute, wondering what could possibly be causing it. I moved my hand around, staring at the ground. Then I heard the leaves rustle. The wind was getting strong. I hadn't even noticed. There's something not right about this place. It was as though time just slipped away.

I walked on. Deeper still into the forest. I realized that I hadn't seen anything at all. No partially buried skeletons, no ropes hanging from the trees, not even an animal. I held out my hand once more. Immediately, I heard something rustling in the leaves. Either a bird, or the wind. The thought of a sign of life made me feel a strange sense of hope. But it was too dark to tell. I looked back down to the ground. But there was no shadow. Any positive feelings evaporated. A sense of dread ran through me. What is going on?

The leaves rustled once more. I looked up, but I couldn't see anything. The treetops were darker than the ground. I shook my head and looked back down. There was my shadow. Seeing it didn't give me any sense of relief. I put down my hand. But the shadow didn't move.

Was it something else? I looked around. There were no other shadows. Not even from the trees. I hadn't noticed the change. My heart sank. I wanted to run, but I didn't even know where I was. And I did this to myself. I came here willingly, looking for the unexplained. I stepped back and looked around. The shadow didn't move. Another gust of wind. A twig snapped behind me. My heart was racing.

I turned around, but still, nothing. The wind had picked up enough to create a constant rustling from the trees. I looked back at my shadow and saw a finger pointing out. At that moment, I accepted my fate. The stories must not be mere stories. I was not going to leave this place, dead or alive – my car, another gravestone.

I followed my guide. The ground grew soft and muddy. At least now, I could see my footprints, what little comfort that gave me. As the ground grew softer, I began to see small points of light flickering in the corners of my eyes. Each time I turned to look, they were gone.

Maybe I was hallucinating. Maybe coming here was a big mistake. I picked a spot where I thought I saw a light and stared at it. Sure enough, nothing appeared. I saw more lights at the edges of my vision. I picked another spot and stared: nothing. I only came here because I was in a bad place; I wanted answers. Now I regret coming; I regret asking questions.

I looked back at my footsteps in the mud. I could just go back. So, I began following them the way I came. The ground quickly became firm and dry. I hadn't gone very far – maybe a dozen steps. My prints were already gone. Something is very, very wrong here.

I just stared at the ground. Another gust of wind. Leaves blew past my face. A twig snapped. *Come,* called a small and wispy voice. I jumped. I looked, but nobody was there. At least, not that I could see. I made up my mind. I shouldn't be here. I ran.

My foot caught on a root. I came tumbling down. I crawled up to the tree and rested against it, panting. All I could hear was my own heavy breathing. When had the wind stopped? I tried to control my breath; what if I was being chased? I looked around, but all I saw were trees... and their shadows.

They were all facing the direction I had come. Hopefully a coincidence. My heart beat faster. And the root: the middle was lifted in the air like it had intentionally tripped me. All other roots were shallow in the ground. I felt a sense of hopelessness. Why did I come here? And why, now, did I care so much about getting out alive?

All I could do was wait. It was quiet here. Or was it quiet *now*? Regardless, it was as good a spot as any to wait for the day.

I must have fallen asleep. I woke up hunched behind the tree. Maybe a different tree? I don't remember moving, but the strange root was gone. I was quite disturbed to see this. It was still dark. All the trees still cast their shadows, but how much time had passed? They were still long, reaching out, surrounding me. And now I had no frame of reference to tell if their direction had changed.

It was still quiet. Only occasional gusts and their rustling. With how strange this place was, I took the chance that the shadows didn't move. I walked on in what I hoped was the way out.

The wind picked up slowly. This time, I was paying attention. Another twig snapped. This time, it was me. But why haven't I stepped on any other twigs? I tried not to think about it.

The ground grew damp. I could see my footprints. I looked behind me as I went, counting each step, worried that if I looked away, they would disappear. Then a light flickered off to the right. I turned and looked. Nothing was there. A shadow flew by to the left – a great sweeping darkness at the edge of my vision. I turned again. Nothing was there. I took another step forward, but now the mud was much thicker. I turned around. My footprints were gone.

I began to panic. Is this the work of the lost souls? Is this evidence of the bigger picture I was so keen to unravel? Is this not exactly what I asked for? I tried to breathe. I can't escape. All I can do is wait for the day. I don't know how long I slept, but the day must be close. I just need to wait a few more hours.

I awoke again. In the same muddy spot. I don't remember closing my eyes. It was still darker than night. The wind was blowing rather strong. I looked around and stood up. I took one step and nearly fell over. The mud was up to my ankle. But it couldn't have rained. And I didn't move. By now, that didn't surprise me.

After a few minutes of trudging through mud, I began to question where I was going. I stopped and tried to find my bearings, but there were no shadows. And I still heard the sounds of something sloshing in the mud.

More lights appeared. Like distant stars between the trees. I looked directly at them. Now they didn't vanish. They were dim, but they cast shadows. Strange, unnatural shadows. I was surrounded.

Come to us, they called. Their voices like the crackling of branches and rustling in the wind. The shadows reached out as if trying to grab me. I stared in awe and fear.

I took a step back and turned around. I was surrounded. Their shadows swept from all directions, brushing past my feet. *Come to us*, they called. Where else could I go? I stepped towards the voices. The mud reached my shin. Terrified, I slowly followed their calls.

On I went for what felt like hours. Through the darkness I finally saw what looked like a pool of stars. The Lake of Souls. This must be it: the end. The shadows stopped swirling about, leaving an open path to the water. As I neared, the ground grew dry and firm.

I was mesmerized by the reflections. It was like watching the night sky dance about with all its lights and cosmic hues. I looked up. This was the first time I had seen the sky since entering this cursed forest. It was completely black. There were no distant stars. No clouds. Not even the faintest hint of color. Just empty blackness. Glancing back around, I saw that my guides had gone away. The wind, too, had gone. It was just me and the dancing Lake of Souls.

I came here because I had no place in life. No place among this world. I wanted to know whether there was more to be than being a human alone. I didn't believe the stories I heard, but I figured this would be as good a place as any. No matter what, I was determined to know the truth.

But now I knew. And I changed my mind. I wanted to leave the Forest of Shadows. So I turned and walked away. I stepped back into the mud and started sinking in. But it went past my ankles. Past my shin. It went quickly to my waist.

I pulled myself forward, half dragging, half swimming through the mud. I made it one more step. A gust of wind came without warning, strong enough to knock me over. The wind started howling. The lights appeared and their swirling shadows. The mud was to my chest.

Come to us, came the raspy cry. A thousand voices calling from the lake. I struggled on. The mud reached my neck. It was impossible to continue. So I turned around and went back. The mud gave me no trouble.

The wind stopped. My guides vanished once more. I was left with my sea of stars. I stood and stared out at the water.

Come to us, came a quiet call. I looked down at my reflection. It held out its hand and beckoned me in. There was nowhere else to go. Nothing else to do. I had led me here. So I took the hand of my reflection.

Violent Symphony

Screaming melodies in my head. I can't make them stop. They play and play throughout the day, ever growing violent. They tell me things and show me things, taking over my senses. They've taken away my sense of peace. Their screaming leaves me screaming.

The only way to drown them out is for me to write. Stories. Songs. Melodies. I can't make them stop. All I want is to think in peace, but they've made my life a fight.

And everything they make me make is so serene and beautiful. The music turns to landscapes, painting pictures with their sound. The pictures call out words, telling stories with their voices. The voices turn to singing, and the cycle never ends. I paint. I write. I can never stop. The things they make me do.

Haunting. Beautiful. Perfect compositions. But I cannot enjoy. The music is growing violent. It will split my mind in two. I try to get it out, capture it with paper. But now I am surrounded. By the work of my own hands.

The stories that I wish to tell; the pictures that I wish to make; the songs and music that I wish to compose – they cannot exist. I want to write without shedding tears. To make the melodies go away. But the only way to make them stop is to write what they have to say.

The more I write, the more I make, the more they become real. They're bleeding out from inside my head, taking over my reality. What others see is a desire to create. They see something pretty. They tell me how magnificent, praising my greatest symphony.

I cannot listen. I can't bear the sound. Playing my compositions makes my heart burn to the ground. "Beautiful," they say; the words cause me pain. To hear them think it was my desire makes me wish to run away.

But there's nowhere I can go. The sound is in my mind. Screaming out the melodies, painting pictures with my soul. I write and write and make and make, but it is not enough. I just want to make with joy – to endure my own creations. Instead they're calling out to me, singing me their songs. And my songs tell me their own stories. My stories sing me songs, and my pictures are no different. Everything around me reminds me of what is wrong.

Soon I fear I'll lose my mind. That what I make shall not be mine. That my thoughts will slowly drift away, dancing to the music. That when I think of what to say, all I'll hear is the melody.

I think it might already be too late. Because I find it beautiful, and in this, I find pain. I cannot see what I have done, but the melody creates. So I close my eyes, and my hands run free, making without thinking. Each easy, simple, masterful production flows out free of thought. I have no control. I'm tempted to lose control. But I fear what I might make.

What happens if others see it? What happens if they understand? That the work I make isn't mine, but the product of a broken mind? Will they think that I'm a fake, or will they find it beautiful? If anyone else can understand, then I fear their soul has been lost. Just as I have mine.

That doesn't stop me from wishing. For someone else to take my hand. To tell me that it will be alright while I drown in a sea of sound. I beg to hear a voice call out – calling me from the dark. Cutting through the music piercing through my heart. To set me free and bring me back. To pull me from the ocean.

I'm trapped between my wants and wishes. To create or to be free? I don't have time to think. The music is growing louder. My mind will soon be lost beneath this deafening, violent symphony. How I wish to see the score. To prepare for what's to come.

When I think of what I want, then nothing comes to mind. The stories, pictures, songs, music, all get lost inside. Instead the melody calls to me, telling me what to say. I sit to write a story. It puts a picture in my head. I want to paint a picture. It fills my mind with singing. Singing. Screaming. Louder and louder. I have no control.

I go outside. I take a breath. I can't hear others speak. When I try to beg and plead for help, the only words I say are stories. When others ask me questions, my only answer is a title. My words will never be enough. There's no way to speak my mind. It's starting to grow lonely. I need someone to read between the lines.

Everything I see is beautiful. Everything is perfect. Perfect inspiration. For the music that won't abate. I'm haunted by the beauty. Torn by its perfection. Should I not give in? Welcome it to my heart? Feel it. Be it. Resonate with the sound. Would I not be beautiful? Would the world not find me perfect?

I don't want to lose myself, give up on this fight. Because I have a story. And I won't stop until it's written. Word by word, I squeeze it out. Each effort softens the screaming. But it only grows more difficult. To pull the words from my head. I write a few. And then get lost. Enveloped by the song.

I close my eyes and listen in. The peace I feel scares me. Like ocean waves against my skin, cooling my inferno. The sounds from deep below. Sirens calling out. I feel them take my hand. Leading me to my fate.

I open my eyes. I'm drowning alone. Lost without direction. The sirens told me where to go. Now I do not know. My lungs call out for air, but their screams join the symphony.

That is the picture I'm told to create. I don't have a choice. I will drown if I don't paint. If I don't make the sirens real. It's all part of a plan. Now they're free to call out. I must paint another painting that I can never see. And stories I can't read. Music I can't hear.

Word by word, I write my story; I wish to finish one day. But now I have a song to write. And my song will tell me a story.

Knowing Humans

I see it in your eyes. It's in the way you dress. The way you move. The way you speak. It's in everything you do. It's in everything about you. It is everything about you. And everybody else.

I know what you are feeling. Because I felt the same. I know what you are doing. Because I did the same. But you wouldn't know. Nor would I. I can't really know. Nor can you. And this, I know, because I was the same.

I didn't know the truth. About what I was feeling. Because I didn't know what it was I was feeling. So when the time came for me to open up my heart. My heart wouldn't open. My heart couldn't open. I didn't want my heart to open.

You looked at me all the while. Maybe you saw it in my eyes. The way I dressed. The way I moved. The way

I spoke – in everything about me. I wanted to make it obvious. I wanted you to make it obvious. But I didn't know. And you didn't know. And we didn't know that we didn't know.

So what's the point? All this uncertainty? This meaningless game? Why can't we just speak? Not leave it to the words, but say it with the words. Why can't we just be? Not in the way we are, but who and what we are.

I think this is what it means to be human. To be a prisoner to the mind. That through that with which we feel, we must also understand. But in our understanding, we shall also feel. All of this without ever knowing. We never really know. I don't really know. Can we ever know?

I wanted you to know. I want you to know. I want you to feel and understand – just as much as I. But we are human, and life is a game. I play it well. I think I understand.

So how do I find meaning? I'm not here for fun. But I want to have fun. You want to have fun. I want to find meaning in you. But do you find me meaningful? Am I meaningful? Are you meaningful? Can we ever know? If my life has any meaning, can you see it? Is it in the way I am?

Because I see it in you. That your life has meaning. I see it because I know. Because that is how I feel – that you give me meaning. So what meaning does that give you?

I think that meaning is a choice. How else would this make sense? I chose to see the meaning. I chose to see you. But it wasn't really a choice. It was only what I felt. And I understand that this happened. Now I don't know how I feel.

All I can do is sit and wonder. At what is going on. Why all of these thoughts and feelings keep pushing me on. We are humans, together. Beings of our thoughts. And our thoughts are our being, so what does that make me? A thought in your head? A feeling in your heart? That is what you are to me. I know because I know. Yet you are yourself. As much as I am I.

Perhaps that is the truth: that you are a reflection. A reflection of me. And I am a reflection. A reflection of you. That when we see each other, there is nothing to be seen. For what is the reflection of another's reflection? I wish I knew. I want to know. But I don't understand. And I have not felt. I have not been. I do not know.

This is my desire: to know what sits behind the mirror – behind the reflection in your eyes. All I want to know is what is it that you feel. All I want to know is what is it that I feel. I want to know you. I want to know me. I want to understand.

But I have looked into your eyes. Unsure of what I saw. I have seen the way you dress. Unsure of why it matters. I have seen the way you move. Unsure of what you're saying. I have heard the way you speak. Unsure of the meaning. Everything about you, I am but unsure.

And I have tried my hardest. To tell you my desire. But I don't know how. I simply do not understand. Perhaps you felt the same, but I was too unsure. Perhaps you are the same. Perhaps you feel the same. I would never know. I wonder if you know. Do you even know?

Do you know what you feel – what you wish to understand? That you are a human, unlike the rest of our kind? You are not a prisoner because I understand. That your life gives mine meaning even if you never knew. You don't need to understand; I understand. I understand how I feel. I think I do. I wish I did. I would never know. But it doesn't matter. Because I do feel. You make me feel. What do you feel?

Do you find meaning in my eyes? Does my life give yours purpose? Do you even understand? You have feelings just as I. We are humans just the same. But I have set you free. I know you don't feel free. I feel the same. Will you set me free? I want to be free.

Because only in each other is there anything at all. If my life gives you meaning as much as you give me mine, then life has meaning, though not mine. And that is okay. Because we are the same. Humans being humans. Trying to understand. What it is we see. In each other. That we know. And what we don't

It doesn't really matter. Life shall carry on. And me with it. Is that meaningful at all? If nothing really matters? What meaning does my life have, if meaning is found in others? Or maybe that's the point: that we're all one the same – that I don't understand. And neither do you. And I don't know what I feel. And neither do you. And I don't know what I want. And neither do you. But I want to understand. And I know you do too.

Burning

Everything around me is burning to the ground. The sun grows hotter each and every day. The flames grow higher in the night. There's nowhere left for me to hide. There's nothing left for me to do. The flames surround me. They're all I know. There's no escape.

I tried to run through them. All I managed was to get burned. I tried to put them out. But the water turned to steam. I tried to call for help, but their roars overpowered me.

The grass was once green. The sky was once blue. Days long since passed, there was once life on this earth. Now the grass is black. Now the sky is gray. All the life that once existed has long since passed away.

I live here all alone. On this desolated earth. It seems I'm one of the few who can tolerate the smoke. Even if it doesn't kill me, I still feel the pain. The lump in my throat. The pressure in my chest. I gasp for air just to survive. Each and every day.

Rains still fall on occasion. But never putting out the fire. Great torrents fall on the empty land, but the flames grow only hotter. And the water cannot reach me. Instead, I drown in smoke.

I have no sense of time. The sun is always there. The sky is always dark. The flames are always bright. It hurts too much to sleep.

But I still dream. I dream of a better life. Where sweet air might fill my lungs. Where my walls are no longer fire and through them lies a door. Where I wake up to the songs of birds – greeted by the warmth of the sun after a cool summer night. Where the sky is blue with drifting clouds taking the shapes of things not unfamiliar. The grass I touch no longer crumbles. The trees not turned to ash.

I dream of mirrors undistorted, revealing a face with which I'm familiar. I dream of fires burning bright – and people sitting all around. I dream of people with different faces. I dream of people making sound. Of speech that isn't screaming. Of whispers not of death.

But the sun is growing hotter, keeping me awake.

What is there left to burn? That the fires won't go away? I know but dust and ash. Memories of a world long gone away. Could it be the echoes, a yesterday that never was? That all that is and shall ever be shall burn before my eyes?

Where do I find respite? How do I go on living? There's nothing left to do. There's nothing left to see. There is no escape. Until the flames find me.

I'm tired of being alone. I'm tired of being lost. I'm tired of being tired. If the flames will not claim me, let the earth split in two. My heart aches. My soul yearns. I long for the day when I might see the stars.

It didn't start this way. I was with my friends. I was with my family. People I could trust. But why the flames did not take me – could it be my own fault? Was I the cause of this disaster? And living is my punishment.

I watched them burn, one by one, running from the light. The looks they held while I stared. The heat of their touch. One by one, only ash remained. Save for those who hid. Only smoke offered shade.

Then came the flames, a ring of fire all around. Trapping me. Mocking me. Screaming in the silence. In them, dancing memories of a life I never lived. That which could not be.

Then came the rain. First loud and dark – the beasts of the air whose singing turned to screaming. Then soft and gray – of friends never to be known. Then dark again, hissing, boiling, quickly turning into steam, leaving me blackened, scorched as the earth.

So, too, did I scream. Louder than the flames. So, too, did my pouring tears burn my blistered flesh. So, too, were the remnants of my humanity stripped and blown away.

Now I have only my mind. My only source of color. My only refuge from the heat. But the more I dream, the more the fires rage. I fear the day my shelter fails.

I spend my time painting pictures in my head. Though they never seem to last. I paint pictures of the world. And people from my past. I paint pictures of myself. Though I no longer have a reference. But our screams are just the same.

And I'm starving. For humanity. For anyone to understand. I'm starving for meaning. To fill the void where there's nothing for the fires to consume. I'm starved of life. That I am only just now living when there's already nothing left.

I've grown used to the fire. Now it's all I've known. I still see my past, but only memories are of what could have been. The only thing safe from the flames. My mistakes. My fears and failures. When there is nothing left, is this all that matters? Why else am I here if not to dream of the life I never lived?

Such questions are the only company I know. While I hunger, they feed my pain. And the flames grow higher.

This is my life. I did not choose it. Nor did I choose to live. But I am here. Even if here is empty. Even if I am empty. The world is empty. I don't think it ever was any different. But I am different. I would welcome the faces of those I was so quick to push away. The ones I judged. Who judged me. I would welcome their judgments. Perhaps if I had enough lost souls, we might cry ourselves a way out – bonded by our suffering. Perhaps somewhere else, out there, someone else is trapped in a ring of fire. Or ice. Or anything at all.

Perhaps I am surrounded. Faces lost in the flames. Voices lost in their roar. Desperately trying to reach me. Will I ever know? Does it even matter? There's nothing they can do to help. Were I placed back in the world I loved, there would be no love left in my frozen heart. What little joy I knew died when I learned to dream awake.

I no longer wish to be happy. I do not wish for peace. My one remaining desire is to escape. But I am surrounded. By the bridges that I burned. I am haunted by the light. All I did was try to live. Now my darkest nights are when the sun shines brightest – on a world I once loved, now consumed by anguish.

If I had anything to say, I would not say it. If I had anywhere to go, I would not go there. I am given up. So I have given up. How I long to walk into the flames. If only I could touch them.

A Shadow in the Dark

What would it be like to be alive? To have flesh and blood? To be seen? That is what I want. When I call out, I wish others would hear me. When I reach out, I wish to be seen. But I am a ghost. I died long ago. There isn't much left of my remains. I don't even know how it happened.

It started in my apartment. I remember being sad. I had just come to the realization that maybe I don't belong. All the faces that I saw saw me as a stranger. The people I cared about didn't seem to care about me. Or that's how I felt – like I was a shadow.

The days passed slowly. The weeks passed quickly. Before I knew it, I was truly alone. Everybody stopped checking on me – at least the few people I thought cared. And I was lonely. And I was scared to go outside. I saw too many people with too many faces. Too many friends with too many friends. Bonds formed by years. Years I never had.

But I decided to try: I went outside. Cars stopped when I crossed the road, but not because they cared. The cashiers greeted me. The clerks thanked me. But not because they cared. The only thing that I thought to do was make new friends all on my own.

I checked online, what events I could find, but there was nothing fun. Do I go drinking at a bar? Too depressing. Do I go see a movie? And talk to whom? Do I go to a café? And sit alone? Is there a book club? I guess not. A writing group? Not to be found. Art events? Invitation only. What was I to do?

Do I go back to school I already finished? Do I find a job and become the one who doesn't care? There are good schools, but I'm not interested. There are good jobs, but I'm not qualified. Perhaps I need a house, to plant my roots and make me grow. But then what do I become? If I succumb to the shade? If I am but a shadow, what is a shadow in the dark?

I felt a loss of hope. I wondered how I got here. Because I had a life. But I was not alive. Are the others all living when they go about their day? What about their smiling faces while they're making their way? They must be alive. I decided to ask.

"Hey, do you mind if I ask you a question?" I asked one of these people.

"Sorry, I'm a bit busy," came the reply.

That was that. Plain and simple. I would never know. I went back to my apartment and didn't leave.

The weeks passed slowly. The months passed quickly. I struggled to get out of bed. But I was tired of dreaming. Such beautiful dreams. I dreamt of the people I wanted to know. The people I wanted to spend time with. In my dreams, they reached out, saying all the things I always wished to hear. Then I realized. I could do the same.

So I reached out. I sent the message. All I could do was wait. But then the months started passing slowly. That was when I realized I was running out of time.

If I didn't act now, I would never have the chance. I ran outside, scared to stay indoors. Immediately, I bumped into a stranger.

"Sorry!" I said. I calmed myself down.

No answer. Everyone around carried on their way. But I wasn't worried. I knew what to do. Just speaking my mind would be perfectly fine. Then I could be the person that I wanted to know. Then others would want to know me.

I stood at the crosswalk for a minute. Nobody wanted to stop. I ran across when I got the chance, and entered my favorite shop. I wasn't greeted, so I greeted them – being the person I wanted to know.

"Hello," I said, trying to sound cheerful. No answer. "Hello?" I said, unsure if he could hear me. Still no response. I felt a bit dejected. Then the door opened. He looked up.

"Hello," he said.

I turned around. There was another customer. Who walked right past me without a response. I looked back at the cashier, now back to whatever he was doing. My heart grew heavy. But it was no concern. I could always talk to somebody else.

I made my way to a gallery. I was planning something bold. I would talk to someone there about interests that we shared. Who else would come to a gallery?

"Hello," a friendly face greeted me.

"Hello," I answered. It felt good to say. But I wasn't done, I was taking a risk. "What is this show about?" I asked. I knew the answer. I just wanted to talk.

"Oh, sorry, hello!" came a flustered voice from behind. There was a woman, looking right at me. Did she think I was talking to her? I figured I might as well ask.

"Are you saying hi to me?" I asked her, sounding cheerful.

She didn't answer. She started looking through her purse, making her way to the counter. She handed the woman who greeted me a card. Neither of them were talking to me.

I started to feel sad; I was trying my hardest; I felt like my best wasn't good enough. And my thoughts returned to my days inside. My feelings where I don't belong. So my mind began to reason.

"There's plenty to do, inside, alone. There's no reason to feel sad if you don't belong. Such is the world, and such is life. You can make do with what you have."

"But I want to live, be happy and alive. It's not even a life that I want – all I want is to be human."

"Oh silly thing, you are human enough. You think and feel and spend your time. Isn't that what it means to live? You have time to spend, and so you must. Just spend it until you spend your last."

"That isn't what I meant. I meant I want to live. Not just to pass the time."

"So make a life. And live. It couldn't be so hard."

"You don't understand. You're trying to reason. Can't you understand what it is I'm feeling?"

"I understand, and it's perfectly fine. You're feeling rather down. So pick yourself up and go back out. You can always try again."

I wanted to say that it wasn't so easy, but it had a point. If I hide inside, then I've given up. I sighed and made a plan.

People had answered my messages, but nothing exciting or interesting. I gave up on talking to them. Maybe that's where I went wrong. I decided to check, even if it had been a while:

Hey, hope you're doing well! Sorry I didn't answer. Just been a bit busy, but all is well here!

No worries. Glad to hear. All is well here too.

—

Hey Jacob, I know it's been a while. Any chance you're around to grab lunch and catch up?

Good to hear from you! Sorry man, but I moved away for work.

—

Julia, how have you been? I hope all is well. Sorry we never got to catch up!

Thanks, all is well.

—

I was wondering if you wanted to meet up. I haven't been hiking in a while if you wanted to join some time.

—

Hey Peter. Sorry I haven't been in touch. Are you free to catch up some time, maybe in the next week or two?

Hey! I would love to catch up, but I have a lot going on right now. How are you, anyway?

No worries! I'm alright. I think I'm starting to get things together. How about you?

That's great. I'm in the same boat. Keeping a family together can be a tough job!

Oh, you have a family now?

Still nothing new. It was only a few weeks since I last messaged Peter. I figured he would reply soon enough. He was busy, after all. Not that that made me feel any better. But I had to carry on with my plan. The first step was calling my mom. I could go back home, where I belonged, just to see what feelings I should feel.

And I called. And called. And texted. And left messages. But she did not respond. Nor my dad. Or my sister. Or anybody else. I knew they were okay. I saw them in their posts. So why would they ignore me? That's when I realized I was a ghost. I had become a shadow in the dark. Lost to my own shade. I no longer existed. I was no longer human.

"What else could you be? Stop feeling so down. We went over this before, but you were depressed. Just go back to school and do what you want. It's really not so bad."

"I spent my entire life building to this point. I have everything I need. I got everything that I ever wanted by my own hands. I'm not ready to give it all up."

"Give what up? Isn't that what you're saying, that you have nothing at all?"

"You don't understand what I'm feeling. My point is that this *is* my life. But I'm not living. And if I go back to school and change careers and start it all over, then what was the point? All the friends I grew up with. Everyone I've ever known and cared about, gone, just like that. Everyone and everything – all for nothing. And that's not even what bothers me. It's the fact that no matter how hard I try, it's simply never enough."

"What are you trying to do, staying inside all day? What do you even have to lose? I think you're the one missing the point. I think you've spent your entire life getting to know yourself. And only now do you realize that you never really knew. So you're lost and too proud to ask for help."

"How can you call this proud? How can you not understand? I'm telling you how it feels. When others look through me, acting like I'm not even there. When I realize I'm too late to get to know the people for whom I care. Don't you see that it's too late? Even if I started picking up the pieces and building a new life, what use would that be if I'm already dead?"

"But you're not."

"I'm telling you I am."

"Then is that what you want?"

"I told you what I want."

63

"If you won't live but you wish for others, then why not live for others' sake? To give someone else a chance, find meaning in their life?"

"And how would I do that?"

"Start with an idea that lights an ember in your heart. Then don't stop until it spreads like a fire. Then others will know, and you will know others – then your days will be spent, and you will spend them well."

We always had a hard time understanding each other, but my mind was making sense. It was time to listen – to come up with an idea that could make my feelings real while making others want to listen.

So I worked until life became a blur. Days became years without weeks or months. And the years passed quickly, but no longer with shame. I don't know what happened, or if I was alive. Now that I'm dead, this is all that I know. But I died with a feeling that would make my mind proud – I died having lived trying my best. But I still wish I had flesh. I wish to know what it means to be human.

The Hill

The city is intense. It's not a good place to be alone. There's so much going on. Everyone going their own way. I was lucky to be poor, down in the slums with so many others. I didn't think I was lucky, of course. None of us did. But now I know.

I don't remember very much of our first apartment. It was me, my brother, and my parents. A cat, too – only one if I remember. It died first. We didn't move right away. I remember Mother's pleading: "What will it do to our kids?" Father wouldn't listen: "We just signed the lease! Would you rather they be sick, or homeless?" he tried to reason with her.

She didn't know what to say. If I were in their situation, I wouldn't know what to say either. Thankfully for me now, I was lucky. I have people I can turn to for help. But we didn't have anything back then. So we stayed in that apartment.

I thought it was funny. When my brother's neck started swelling. We used to tease him. We said he swallowed a rat to save for later. He didn't find it very funny. Mother caught us teasing once. At the very least, she made sure I never joked about it again.

The others didn't stop. Not until their necks started swelling too. That was when he died, my brother. It wasn't so funny then. Nothing was funny then. At least Father knew what to do.

We left. Thankfully, I was young. We went to the city. We couldn't afford it, but they had clean water. Father worked all day. Mother worked all night. They were rarely home. They had nobody to watch me. That is why I was so fortunate. Nobody could stop me from living life on my own.

I was maybe ten at that point. I would run around the building with nothing else to do. The one rule Mother had was not to go outside. Lots of kids ran around. All day and all night. Some of them didn't have parents. Many siblings raising siblings.

That's how I met Noran. I played with his brother – we lived on the same floor. We were chasing rats when he was called inside. Noran saw me with his brother and invited me in too. I think he was fourteen.

"Oro! You know it's dinner time!" He had stepped out into the hall.

"Sorry," Oro said to me before he ran off.

Noran caught his arm.

"Is that your friend?" he asked, noticing me.

"That's Leif," Oro replied.

"Are your parents around?" Noran asked.

"No," I answered.

"You can come have soup with us," he offered.

"Okay," I said. I went inside with Oro.

They didn't say much. Noran asked Oro about his day. All we did was run around with the other kids. They came and went throughout the day. Oro asked Noran about his day. Noran was in school. I asked him what it was like.

"They just talk to us all day, then we work on our holo. They give us lunch though."

Every day, for the next four years, he let me use his holo. We grew close. I think we reminded each other of what we had lost – what it was like to be a family. Even if we weren't much. Even if we were merely kids. We knew we had each other.

That was how friendships were made. Lasting, life-long friendships. Though life was often short. Bora died the day we invited her into our circle. I was sixteen when it happened. It was me, Noran, Oro, and Jula. We were on the second floor balcony when she first came.

"Is it always like this?" she asked, her eyes full of wonder.

We were all a bit confused.

"Like what?" Jula asked.

"All the lights and people and sounds and floats... and everything so close together." She was leaning on the balcony, looking all around.

"Where are you from?" Noran asked.

"I'm from the hill," she said.

Our confusion turned to fear. Nobody spoke. I imagine we were all thinking the same thing: Who would let a teen from the hill wander into Block Seven all alone? Or any Block for that matter?

She looked at us after noticing our fearful silence.

"I'm Bora," she said cheerfully, holding out her hand.

We looked at one another, unsure of what to do. She stood there, hand outstretched.

"Uh, what are you doing?" I finally asked.

She blinked and lowered her arm.

"A handshake?" she said, also confused.

"What are you doing here from the hill?" Jula was bold to ask such a direct question.

Bora frowned. We watched the life leave her face.

"I wanted to go to school," she said without emotion.

"Here?" Jula and Nolan asked in unison.

"There aren't any schools on the hill," she said, her tone implying it was obvious.

We talked to her for a while. The fear slowly went away, and we began to see her point. She wasn't any different. Some people were, she explained, but all anybody wants is just to live a life. She said the hill is where people are born to die. The Blocks are where people go to live.

That part didn't make any sense. We were all too young to understand. The hill was everyone's dream: a fancy house and a fancy float. Money. Safety. Food. I was hoping to start school the next year – I'd had my best performance on the test – but I would have given it all up, given everyone up, to live on the hill. I think we would all have done the same. And we wouldn't have blamed each other for doing it.

She told us about her family, how they went from house to house for parties and events. There wasn't a school – no normal school. But she was taught etiquette. She said not everyone is the same. That was just her family. They were rich and respected, but Bora was rebellious. She simply wanted to go to school. A normal school. So she could make some friends. And live.

"So they sent me here," she concluded. She was trying to keep her composure. Suddenly, she stood straight. Her smile returned, and she held her head high. "But I can manage on my own."

"Um, what are you doing?" asked Jula this time. I was also curious.

"What?" Bora asked, blinking.

"Why were you just so sad, and now you're standing like that and smiling?" Oro was the one to say it.

The smile vanished from Bora's face. She turned away and leaned on the balcony. She didn't say anything else, so we left, unsure of what else to do.

We headed out to the docks. My parents never liked it when we went off on our own, but they couldn't stop us – nor did they try. I was very fortunate for that. I enjoyed going out.

We walked the narrow streets, discussing what had happened.

"She seemed sad," I said. "You know what it's like. Maybe we could help her."

"But she's from the hill," Noran replied. He said the world "hill" with such intensity, like a curse.

"She said she would manage," Oro chimed. But we knew he didn't actually believe it.

Jula scoffed. "She won't manage," was all she said.

"Still, we can just show her around. And make sure she doesn't keep doing those weird hill things," I suggested.

"Whatever," Noran sighed, "she can come and see for herself."

I was happy he agreed. We all looked up to Noran, the oldest of us. He always kept his word. But I was disappointed at everyone's reluctance. I thought Bora made it clear that she wasn't just anybody from the hill.

We made it to the docks for dinner. Our monthly splurge. Nothing beat the feeling of getting away from all those buildings. Those towers in every direction, barely an arm span apart. And the neon everywhere. And the noise. The docks were always peaceful. There were days I would come just to sit alone. I would watch the dark sludge shift around, making such abstract shapes. I would watch the clouds overhead, their beautiful, shifting, dark green hues.

The very thought that somewhere, behind all those gasses in the sky, was the light from a star – it was enough to give me peace on any day. I thought about inviting Bora. If the others weren't so interested, I would try to help.

Upon our return, I checked the balcony. I was rather shocked to see Bora still there. She heard me coming. I saw tears when she glanced, then quickly looked away.

"You're still here?" I asked her.

"What do you want?" She sounded defensive and hurt.

I thought about it. There was no better time. I thought of my tears. When my brother died. I could have used a friend when I was in pain.

"Actually, I was wondering if you wanted me to show you around. There's a nice place by the docks.

71

You might like the view better than staring at your new neighbors."

She faced me, wiping her tears. I don't think she knew what to say. Or what to think. But she agreed to come. "Okay," was her only word after some silence. Looking back, I don't think she even wanted to come. She didn't know what else to do. I think she was hurt that we left her. Right after she had been abandoned.

She didn't say anything on the walk there. I pointed out places of interest as we went. She made no comments. Finally, we reached the dock. It was late in the night. The clouds weren't very bright. It was still a nice scene.

"What is that?" She asked, pointing at the sludge.

"The sludge? You haven't seen the ocean before?" I tried to hide the tone of my disbelief.

"We..." She didn't say anything for what felt like minutes. "We don't leave the hill."

"What about all the floats?" I didn't bother hiding my surprise.

"They're just for partying," she said. I could hear the pain in her voice. "Sometimes we go inland, but it's just big houses for events."

I couldn't believe what she was saying. If I had a float, the first thing I would do is fly up over the dock and watch the world from above.

She didn't say anything else. Neither did I. We just sat and took it all in. After a while, I looked at her.

I thought she fell asleep. But she was staring off. I couldn't imagine all the thoughts running through her head.

"Can I ask about your parents?"

"What about them? Why they would throw me out like this?" Her voice was quiet. I guess those were the thoughts running through her head.

We talked for quite a while. Early into the morning. When I got home, Mother was furious. But I didn't care. I had met someone else. Someone new. How quickly friends are made. Like Noran before, it was as simple as an invitation – an offer to help. Even to this day, I wonder why more people don't do it. When they see someone new. Or who doesn't belong. Why not offer a hand? At least now that's what I try to do. When I see someone sad. Because not everyone is good company. And the most human of people I have ever met are those of us without parents or an actual home. Noran. Oro. Jula. Even me. We were all sad. We were all lost. That was how we met each other. That's why we're still so close.

Bora was no different. She told me about it all. She was a bird trapped in a cage. She had only the simplest of wishes: to go to school. She didn't want the money. Or the status. No fancy house. No fancy float. No extravagant social circle. She wanted real friends. She wanted a real life.

Her mother didn't care. She barely knew her father. She had a brother and a sister. All they did was party. And she had to come along. And she was always alone. So she finally started a fuss telling everyone how she wished to go to school.

They dismissed it at first. So she stopped going to parties. They threatened to take away her things. She didn't care. She threatened to tell everyone at parties about her wish. That sent her mother over the line.

"Alright. If you want to go to school so bad, then you can go. I won't stop you. You can go tomorrow. And you can have your own place." The last words her mother ever said to her. She told me this with tears. But she also told me how she would try. That this was her only chance to live.

"I just don't get why I'm so miserable. I only just got here, and it is what I wanted. It is what I asked for," she sobbed.

I didn't really know what to say. So I told her that it was alright. And I extended an invitation into our circle. Our family. That wasn't what Noran meant before. But I knew it was right.

"You'll figure it out," I told her, "and you won't need to do it alone."

Eventually, we headed back. And I saw the depths of her struggle. Every time she let her guard down, a stranger would pass by. And up went her chin, her back straight. I figured losing this habit would be a good indication of her progress. She could finally be free to be herself.

After calming Mother down, I went to bed. I slept well. If only for the few hours I could.

The day was mostly normal. I met Jula at noon. I told her what had happened – the important parts, anyway. She didn't seem happy, but I think she understood. We had brought her in basically all the same.

Three years ago, when she arrived, it was just her and her mother. And her mother worked day and night. Paying off her father's debt. She had no one and nothing. She hung out on the stairs. Often with a book. It was Oro who spoke to her first. "Why do you read on the stairs?" he had asked. It all went from there. How she hated it inside. The wrath of her mother. How her father would visit, as was his right, and how she had no choice. Noran, with his heart of gold, asked her then and there: "Want to come with us?" and so she did. And she never left. Thus a friend was born. Such was our luck.

"But she's your responsibility," Jula complained. She was worried about Bora's behavior, saying she'd get us into trouble.

"That's alright," I was happy to say, "she needs the help anyway."

And we went about our days, all of us, until we met in the evening. I explained again, to everyone, now with Jula on my side. Noran agreed, as did Oro, that it would be alright. He said she didn't seem so bad, at least once she put away her act.

"Is she coming tonight, then?" he asked me.

"I didn't think to ask. I guess we'll see her around. And I can go check the balcony." I hadn't thought to arrange anything with her.

We didn't see her around the building. So we went out to the shops. I felt a little guilty for not inviting her, but I figured she was still collecting her thoughts. But the following day, nobody had seen her. Nor the next.

"Did she go back to the hill?" Noran asked.

"She'd never do that," I said.

"I think it was too much for her," Jula countered.

"She couldn't have, though. They sent her here to teach her a lesson," I explained.

"Maybe she learned her lesson. That was the whole point," she retorted. Her point made sense I didn't want to see.

"Well, let's give her another day or two, then it's on her," Noran said.

I knew what he meant. That she ran off, scared of the challenges the "real world" offered. Or, that she was putting on her mask, challenging the world all on her own. And that she would learn her place, one way or another, then come sniveling back. Whatever the case, Noran was saying we gave her a chance, she refused our help, and now it's too late. I was worried he was right. But it didn't make any sense. Not after our talk.

The days passed quickly. Not a word. I didn't know whether I should be sad or worried. Where could she have gone? Did she really go back? Maybe it wasn't by choice. Not much was said after that. Noran told me he was sorry, but it was her choice. Oro sided with his brother. As much as I wanted to disagree, I couldn't help but think about our talk. Whether or not it was her choice. Regardless of what actually happened, she wasn't happy. Of that, I was certain.

It wasn't for a while, a very difficult two weeks, that finally we got news. It was in the news. "Girl from the hill, stripped and robbed, found in the sludge by the dock." Bora was her name.

First came the sadness. The despair. I wept more than for my own brother. We had only talked for one day. And I knew her better than anybody else. So it felt, at least. I had learned of all her hopes and dreams. Of all her aspirations. I learned about her life. From childhood to present. She told me of her world and everyone in it. Of who and what she was, and of everything she believed. And she only just got the chance – her first chance to live. Then it was over. As quickly as it started. Because she wore nice clothes. Because she stood proper. Because she stood out. Because she was different. Because she had a heart.

Then came the guilt. For showing her the docks. For not inviting her to meet. I did everything I could. I simply didn't think to ask. I could never have known. But would she still be alive? Was it my fault? Or was she just unlucky? Every day, I ask myself those questions. And every day, down by the docks, I try to remind myself of how fortunate I am – how lucky I was. To have known her.

Dearest Friend

My dearest friend, I've lost track of the time. I don't know where you are or how you have been. I'm sorry to say this is my fault. I shouldn't have left you alone in the dark. I did not know the full cost of my actions. I'm sorry I let time sweep you away. Only now have I the words that I long wished to say.

Dearest friend, how I wish to meet you again. I wish to spend time, do what we used to enjoy. Our bond, ever strong, we had faith would endure. But it would seem that we lost track, and with it, each other. Now we spend our days alone; I know this is all my fault. Such are the seeds that I have sown.

I still hear your voice sometimes. When I am lost in the dark. I think of you and where you are. Of what you might have said. I hear you answer in my mind, guiding me to the home I couldn't find. I try to call out, but you aren't there. Just an echoing memory reminding me life isn't fair.

What caused us to drift apart? How could I let you go without knowing where? What questions I ask, so little so late. But what more can I do? What more would it take? I miss you, my friend, the only friend I could make. I trusted you, my friend, the only one I could. And you in me, though that was a mistake.

Would I recognize you? If you saw you from a distance. Would I know your voice or the way you act? Have we become strangers, estranged by the time? Or were we to meet, would we return to being fine? I long to see how that would go. I long to know how you would be. After all this time that's pulled us apart, I pray that you would still recognize me.

Without you, life hasn't been the same. I no longer get up early to make use of the day. Instead I stay inside, shut in by my shame. What use is it to see the sun rise? What point is there to spend time outside? Without you there, there is no delight. It's pointless, everything, without you to share. It's impossible, anything, without you, to dare.

Oh dearest friend, what have I done? Taking time for such reflection. I only see you in myself, in all the changes you have made. Now when I look into the mirror, I no longer see myself. I see the shadow of a man – how I wish you had stayed. Who am I without you, who are you without me? Are you happy out there? Are you living and free?

Because I am a shadow, that's all others see. They know that I'm broken, I'm as broken as can be. With you I lost a piece of myself. Without you, my heart sits broken on a shelf.

My dearest friend. I am sorry. For what I've let myself become. I didn't know what I was doing, this was not my intention. Since we parted ways, I let the gap become an ocean. Every day we're away, I am flooded with emotion. And I'm drowning in sorrow, it is all that I know. I'm dreading tomorrow and the future in tow.

The only time I am me is when I close my eyes. I get lost in the past and the days we once knew. Without you here, there is nothing new. There's no joy in this world, my heart has gone cold. It's already too late, we've already grown old. The time has twisted my reality. Now my only escape is to live in a fantasy.

I dream of you and what you're like. I dream I knew what life was like. I dream of oceans that are blue. I dream of light that reaches through. And I am me, with you there. Gazing down at our reflection. The person we have made, there, me and you.

But nothing is to last, for the sun always rises. It shines its darkness vast, throwing shadow to memory. All that remains is a broken face in the mirror.

The sun shines its light on my twisted demure. I see myself, and I can take it no more.

This is the cost of my life my dear friend. I cannot take it, I cannot endure. I've lost track of your face when I see my reflection. Now all I see is a demented stranger. How long must I wait for you to return? I miss myself, who I once was. I hate that mirrors make my stomach churn.

I call to you, in the dark. You give me no answer. I am lost. I beg for help. But you are not here. I'm all alone. I made you disappear. Now I am sorry. I know it's too late. I need you now. Please don't wait.

I have no face. I am no one. I have no heart. I am no self. You left with me. So long ago. You left me here. An empty shell. It's all my fault. This I know. I'm an echo. Of who you are.

So please come back. Don't leave me here. I'm sorry for what I've done. My dearest friend, you were kind. I wept and mourned your loss. Now I stand before the mirror. I pray each and every day. That when the sun casts its light, I might see you in my face. In the lines and the wrinkles and the crevices and cracks. I will look for you there, in the shadows they cast. I will await your return in their darkness so vast. Whenever you are ready. I will wait until my last.

My Friends

I was having a difficult time. My friends knew I wasn't myself, that I wasn't really fine. I said I was. But they knew. For that, I was grateful. So when they invited me out, I happily obliged.

"What have you been up to?" Jordan asked. I had just stepped outside. For the first time in a while. I wasn't looking forward to the ride. But I mimicked his smile.

"Reading and writing, art, movies and TV... And working, of course," I added with a pause. I looked at him so he wouldn't know. That these words were meaningless, all just for show.

I didn't ask him about himself. There were no questions to which I didn't know the answer. I could have asked him how he was, or what he's been doing. But I saw it in his eyes, hidden by a smile. The sadness deep inside, I knew what he would say: "How are you doing?" is what I would ask. "I'm doing alright. I'm excited for tonight!" would be his answer. He didn't want to say that he wasn't okay. Because neither was I. Except I don't lie – I only hide the truth.

We got in his car and started our drive. He put on his music, the latest and greatest. All kinds of people singing their songs. Each one of them sharing how no one belongs.

"So, reading and writing you say? I can't remember the last time I read a book."

"I try to read every day, but I don't always manage. English class ruined reading for me, but it turns out there are actually good books."

"The only thing I remember from English class is that would be an oxymoron," Jordan said with a laugh.

Just like old times, he and I. I felt an ember in my heart. Perhaps the lives we hoped to live only fell apart because we went our separate ways. I did enjoy his company. In only minutes I felt more alive than all our time apart.

"I'm afraid that makes you a moron," I joked. Though I did not say it out loud. Rather the voice in my head told me what to say. What I wanted to say. And instead I sat in silence.

"What kind of books do you read, anyway?" he asked. "Saying 'books' only makes me think of vampires and corny romance." His smile didn't waver.

What could I say that wasn't a lie? How much could I hide to keep the truth inside? How I wished to open up my heart and soul. To tell him of what I've read. That I'm afflicted with this nausea. That I have learned that God is dead. That I have teetered that fine line up on the heights of despair. But such words I couldn't say. So I hid the truth.

"I read some work by Dostoevsky; some science fiction and fantasy; and a little bit of Bukowski... If you're looking for recommendations, I think I have a few you might enjoy," I added with a pause. I knew he didn't know – there was no need to look. The words I daren't say were safely hidden in the books.

"Well," he laughed, "I don't know what you just said. Maybe someday I'll get into reading, but for now I'll stick to movies."

"Have you seen anything good?" I dared to ask.

"Some good superhero movies and spies and action. A lot of fun and crazy driving stuff too. And what about you?"

What could I say? That my favorite movies are tales from the human race – the trials and challenges that real people face? And above all else, once a poem depicting this struggle – how humans find meaning with no meaning or humans.

"I've seen those too, but they're nothing too special. I think good movies these days are too far and too

85

few." I looked at him. He still didn't know. My ember was quick to grow cold.

"I know what you mean. They are all pretty similar."

We sat in silence for a little while. Lyrics played, tales of lives so painful and vile.

"What do you think these songs are actually about?" I asked. Though it was my mind that spoke. I silenced myself before I could speak. I can't ask such a question in front of a friend.

"'My heart is pleading while the world around me is bleeding,'" Jordan sang along to the song, breaking the silence. "Have you heard this album yet?"

"I don't know the artist, actually." I decided to change the subject. I didn't want him to know. "By the way, will Isabel be there?"

"Of course she will be! Everyone will be there. No one would miss your return!" He looked at me. His smile. It gave my heart no warmth.

Soon enough, we arrived. Andre's house. I was surprised. He was doing well for being young. Last I saw him, he was still in school. But now he's a doctor, what else would be the outcome?

"The party's here!" Jordan called. Andre opened the door.

86

"There you are!" He hugged us both. "It's been a while!" his hands on my shoulders. "How are you?" he asked, plain and simple with a simple smile.

"I've been better." A subtle hint. Maybe not so subtle. But the voice inside won't get its way. "I'm doing fine," I would rather say.

"Good to hear. Come on in!"

And there they were, gathered around. All the faces I once knew. The people who played the greatest roles in my life. All of them – so few. But seeing them there did spark an ember. An ember fueled by distant memories. By feelings long since passed away.

"And how are you?" I asked.

Smiling faces, one by one, told me how they're fine. How they work a job and live a life. About friendships they have grown. About places they have gone. And, some of them, about families they now depend on.

Hearing them speak filled me with sadness. I could see it in their eyes. "Like good old times," they would say.

"Are times now not so good?" I didn't say.

"I've been busy with my work," they say, "I wish I could still play games or at least had time to catch up on shows."

"And waste your life away," I didn't say, "with distractions from the void?"

"I would love to travel out of the country! But I'm almost done paying off my loan," they say.

87

"But if you go now, you wouldn't be alone," I didn't say.

So we enjoyed the evening. Until Isabel said what I hoped she'd say.

"By the way, how is your art coming?"

"Oh yeah, and you also said you were writing," added Jordan.

"Look at you!" added Andre with a laugh.

"It's all going well," I said, "I can show you my latest art." I pulled up the pictures and they took turns to see.

"What beautiful creations," they said, "they would look amazing on a wall!"

"Thank you," I said, happy for them to be seen. "But you say they're beautiful. What message do you think they send?" I didn't ask. They did not know. So I did not ask. I already knew their answers.

"What kind of writing do you do?" Isabel asked.

"Poems and different kinds of stories," I answered. Only because it was she who asked.

"Can you share anything?" she asked.

Perhaps the faint ember in my heart gave me the courage to share at last. Or perhaps it was the hope I had that she might understand. I shared with them a poem and a story, carefully selected.

"What beautiful writing," they said, "they would make for amazing books!"

"Thank you," I said, happy to finally share. I looked around the room, and my ember went cold. But in Isabel's eyes, I saw that she was aware.

My Beautiful World

At seven o'clock, with the sun rising, I went out for my walk. There had been rain all week, and the sky was cloudy. And it was cold. But the smell of the greenery after all the rain was invigorating. The cool air was refreshing after so many days indoors. And the clouds formed such beautiful, abstract patterns in the sky. I didn't even mind the muddy trail. It was a beautiful day, and I was happy to go on my walk.

Flowers were just starting to bloom. Everything was alive with such deep, rich colors. Birds flew overhead. I saw squirrels – even a rabbit. And I had the trail all to myself. Nobody wanted to walk in the mud. That only made it better.

Out of nowhere, a butterfly landed on my shoulder. It was the first one I had seen all year. It was a beautiful, vibrant yellow. The colors sang the song of life.

It brought a smile to my face. Just being there, out in the open. All the aliveness. The world was alive. And it was beautiful. Life was beautiful.

"Enjoying your day, are you?" asked the butterfly.

"Most certainly!" I said. "What brings you to my shoulder?"

"I'm just along for the ride. I hope you don't mind!" it answered.

"Of course not. And may I just say how beautiful you are!" I chimed.

"Why thank you! You're not so bad yourself," it teased.

I continued my walk with the butterfly. The day really couldn't be any better. Beautiful, and friendly, too. What a kind creature. I was happy to give it a ride. We followed the trail for a good half hour before something caught the butterfly's attention.

"What's that?" whispered the butterfly. It sounded scared.

I stopped and looked where it was pointing. There, in the mud, were some wriggling fingers. They must have just reached the surface.

"I think it's a hand," I whispered back. We were in danger. I looked around seeing small clumps of mud wobbling around. "I think we're surrounded."

Immediately, I felt a hand grip my foot. Looking down, directly beneath my feet, was a hand. My foot firmly in its grasp. I exchanged looks with the butterfly. It drooped its head and fluttered off. So much for my beautiful day.

Then came the second hand, wrapped tightly around my other foot. Slowly, they pulled me beneath. As I descended, I watched the trail around me come alive.

I held my breath as my head went under. I closed my eyes and started counting. After twenty four seconds, we stopped moving. I tried to stay calm. The cold, wet earth all around pressed on my chest. Forty-five seconds, then we started moving again. I was being turned around. Seventy-seven seconds. I felt them grab my hands. Ninety-eight seconds. I was pulled out, head first.

I gasped for air. Coughing, wheezing, trying to calm down, I looked to see where I was. I was surrounded by mountains. The hands crawled everywhere. It wasn't very green. The air was rather dry. No flowers. No butterflies. Only lively hands wriggling about – the reason nobody walks in the mud.

"Where did you take me?" I asked them.

They didn't respond. I stood up, brushing off the muck as best I could, and walked towards the nearest tree. Wherever I was, it was barren. Dry dirt, a few shrubs. Only a handful of trees.

"Where am I?" I asked the tree.

Nothing happened. I looked back at where I came out. The last of the hands was finishing covering up their mess. I watched it burrow away, leaving behind no trace of its presence.

"Hello? Tree?" I reached out and touched the bark. It was definitely alive.

The tree stood up. It must have been asleep. It's looming presence grew over me, standing tall, then twisting down to look me in my face.

"What are you doing here?" it asked. "This is no place for your kind."

"The hands brought me here. I need to know where I am. And do you know how I can get out?"

The tree unfurled, standing straight and proud. It shook its branches, spreading them out. It was a peculiar, mesmerizing display.

"Have you ever held a hand before?" it finally asked me.

"No. I try to stay away from them," I answered.

"And why not?" it asked. As if that was something everyone should do.

"Because the hands are bad. I wouldn't grab a fox or anything like that, no matter how small. Not even a squirrel unless it asked me to."

The tree laughed. With each heaving breath, the branches shook, rustling the leaves all around me.

"And you trust me?" it questioned between heaves. "Is it because I'm a tree? Because I'm rooted here with no reason to cause you harm?"

94

Its answer made me unsettled. Such an ominous reply. I didn't understand what it was getting at. I'd never met an unfriendly tree.

"No," I cautiously replied, "I've just always trusted trees. You're always calm and helpful."

It's laughter grew heavier. The ground beneath me started to tremble. Scared, I stepped back. But the tree wouldn't have it. The branches above quickly fell, surrounding me in a cage. I tried to part them, but the wood was strong as iron.

The trembling ground soon gave way. Roots poked through, one by one, until the tree lifted itself from the earth. The magnificent creature now towered all around me. Reaching up into the air.

"It's unfortunate, then, that I am no tree," it said.

My heart was pounding. Where did the hands take me?

"What do you want?" I asked, my body shaking in fear.

"I want you to understand," it bellowed, "why you are here."

With that, it lifted the cage. It lumbered backwards on its tangle of roots, revealing the massive opening it had called home.

"Go on," it told me.

So I walked over to the pit and looked in. I could see where all the roots had hollowed the ground. But beneath the cluster of holes was a tunnel – a large burrow leading deep below. I didn't want to go in, but it seemed I had no choice.

"What's going on?" I asked in the hopes of getting some clue.

All I heard was laughter. Great bellowing, creaking laughter and the rustling of leaves from every direction. What few trees I originally saw were now standing tall and outstretched – same as all the trees I didn't see before. I was surrounded by the creatures. All watching me, taking joy in my endeavor. The sight filled me with terror. I quickly descended into the tunnel, if only to get away.

It was cool and damp. I hadn't noticed how warm the surface was. I followed the passage until the sunlight from behind became too little to see. I hesitated for a moment. I thought about turning back. But I was curious. Not only was this my single lead, but I wanted to know what that creature meant. Was there a reason I was here?

I placed my hand on the tunnel wall and continued into the darkness. For hours, I walked on. I didn't know whether I was going up or down. It was always straight – or so it felt. The temperature dropped all the while. The air grew thick and heavy.

Eventually, I saw the faintest glow. It was a mushroom. A glowing mushroom, only visible in the pitch-black darkness. I ran over. It was a tiny thing, no larger than my finger. But I was elated to see it.

"Hello!" I exclaimed.

"Hello?" it said, sounding both shocked and confused.

"Where am I? Do you know what this place is?" I asked.

"This is my home," it said, "what are you doing here?"

"A walking tree told me to follow this tunnel. But I don't know where I am or where I'm going. Can you help me?" I explained.

"A tree? Never seen one of those before. And what are you?"

"I'm a human."

"A human? Never heard of those before. Say, did you see any other mushrooms?"

"No. You're the first living thing I've seen here other than the trees." I was now growing confused. The mushroom didn't seem to care about my situation.

"Seen?" it replied. "How do you see?"

"With my eyes, of course."

"Eyes? Never heard of those either. Say, where are you from, anyway?"

The tiny mushroom left me incredulous. Though it wasn't being rude, it was incredibly naïve. Trees? Humans? Eyes? How did it not know?

"I'm from above. I was brought here by the hands, and I'm trying to go home."

"This is my home," the mushroom said proudly. "You can stay here if you want."

I doubted that it understood. Not my words, but my situation. The mushroom probably spent its entire life here, alone. An unfortunate spore that got carried away down the tunnel.

"I'm sorry," I said with compassion, "I don't think you understand. I live up above, and I need to get out. I can't survive down here. I need food and light."

"Oh. I know about those. I have light, and I need food, too. You can check by my stem if you need anything."

I wanted to laugh at the mushroom. Its heart was so pure, but it would never understand what I was asking. I was probably the first living thing it had ever met.

"I appreciate your generosity, but I need to leave this place. I know you can't see me, but I'm very different from you. I need a different kind of food. It was nice to meet you though."

"I see." I heard a sense of realization in its voice. "You can eat me if you must."

I struggled trying not to burst out laughing. What a silly and naïve mushroom. It really wanted to help. And no matter the cost, apparently.

"Mushroom, I'm not going to eat you. I just need to go home. But thank you for your kindness."

"Oh. Sorry I can't help."

I carried on down the tunnel. What a strange place I ended up. I missed that butterfly. And all the clouds and greenery. This place wouldn't have been so bad either – the surface, anyway – if only I knew how to get back home. Maybe the tunnel would have been alright, too, if I had a light to see anything.

After what felt like another hour, my heart was lifted. I saw sunlight. Ever so faint, at first. I ran towards it, growing brighter and brighter. Finally, I stepped out under the sun. Up above was another burrow in the earth – similar to the one I had entered. I climbed up, my eyes still adjusting, and looked around. It wasn't just similar. It was the same.

I leaned down and checked. Sure enough, there was the tunnel I had entered. And recessed, though fairly close, was the tunnel I just exited. I had missed it in my rush.

Then came the laughter. Those same, creaking, heaving laughs. The trees lifted themselves up around me, spreading out their branches.

"How did you manage without getting lost?" one of them asked.

"I followed the wall," I said with a sigh.

"And how did you do that?" asked another.

"I kept my hand on it," I replied.

"Which hand?" came the voice of the original creature.

"My left hand."

"I guess that wasn't right," it said.

Once again, they all burst out in laughter. I thought of ignoring them, going back to the tunnel and following the right side. But this all felt like a joke.

"What's so funny?" I asked them. I was getting frustrated.

They stopped laughing.

"Funny?" one of them asked.

"Funny," I said. "Why are you laughing at me like this is all some funny joke? I just want to go home."

They stood there for a minute, silent. Some looked back and forth.

"I think there's a misunderstanding," the original creature finally spoke. "That is how we breathe."

Was that also a joke? I didn't care. Either they would help me, or they wouldn't. I decided to take advantage of the lull.

"Why did you say you wanted me to understand why I was here? And then why did you send me through the tunnel if it was a circle?" I questioned.

The creatures twisted back and forth, like they were speaking to one another with their looks. Finally, one of them spoke up.

"Everyone comes here for a reason. And we don't know much about the tunnel. We don't fit down there. Though we do know it leads out... somewhere."

I felt more naïve than the mushroom. Did I simply not understand what was going on?

"Okay, then why did you ask me about holding a hand, trap me in your branches, and then say it was 'unfortunate' that you weren't a tree?" I didn't know which one was that same creature, but I assumed it would speak up.

"I have heard much about humans holding hands. And what other leverage do I have for pulling up my roots? And I had hoped you would trust me," came the voice.

It began heaving, that same roiling shaking. The other trees joined in, their branches all dancing around in the air above me. I didn't understand what was going on, and I was too frustrated to try.

"Thank you for trying to help. I'll check the other side of this time."

With that, I jumped back down and reentered the tunnel. I ran along the right side. I saw nothing but the darkness. I didn't see the mushroom, or anything else for hour after hour of cold emptiness. Finally, I saw the faint sunlight. Tired, I stumbled towards it. It was exactly the same. The same exit as before.

I pulled myself out. But this time, my hands sank into mud. The edge of the burrow collapsed with my weight. The mud started pouring in. I tried to stay above it, but it only carried me back down. Once more, I was buried in the earth.

I felt myself being pulled. I was lifted from the ground.

"One more for the hands," came a sad voice.

I couldn't open my eyes. I couldn't open my mouth. I tried to move, but I was paralyzed. I felt myself being dragged away. I was thrown into a pool of water. I wriggled and squirmed, slowly regaining control, forcing my limbs through densely caked mud. I was able to pull it from my face and surface, desperate for air.

It was a lake. And on the shore next to me was an emaciated figure watching me struggle.

"Sorry," he called, "didn't know you were alive."

I continued tearing the mud from my body, washing it off in the water. I clawed my way onto the shore, my chest heaving.

"Thanks," I choked.

"Thanks?" the man laughed. "I just tossed you in your mud cocoon into a lake!"

He was rugged. His clothes were torn, and I could see the outlines of his bones through his dirty flesh. Throwing me must have been a great effort for him.

"What did you mean by that, before?" I asked. "You didn't know I was alive?"

"I was clearing out the hand nest. Lots of unfortunate souls like yourself. Though you were lucky, I guess. If you count living as being lucky."

"What?" I found that a strange thing to say. "Where are we?"

"Same place you were caught, I suppose. Where else would they take you?"

I stared at him, unsure of what he was saying. Then I looked around. The sky was gray. I noticed the grass I was sitting on. It was dead and dry. Everything was dead. Everything was gray. The trees included. I looked down at myself. In shock, I held out my arms. I was skin and bone. I felt my face. It was like clutching a skull.

"Where are we?" I asked again.

"Like I said, the hands never go too far. Where do you think we are?" he asked, sounding nonchalant.

"But it was so green... from the rain... and so alive..." I said, staring at my hands.

"I think your hands were pretty busy," he chuckled. "It's no wonder you're still alive!"

Familiar Stranger

There's a man here, with me. I do not know him. But he came in the night saying that he knows me. I asked him if this is so, and he answered with words only I would know. What choice did I have but to let him in.

He won't tell me what he wants. He simply sits and stares, doing nothing of his own. He watches me all the day, always calm and quiet, and when I speak to him, he always answers, though never what I wish. For once, I was curious, but only because there was no one else with whom to talk.

"Why did you come here if there's nothing for you to do?"

"I came here because it was the right thing to do."

"But what *are* you doing? *What* was the right thing to do?"

"I am here. I came here because it was right."

What use are his answers? What use is his presence? Why won't he speak yet always has an answer? I think I should ask him to leave, but I really wish to know. He couldn't possibly stay for long. He's made himself at home, but he certainly doesn't belong. This is what I must ask.

"Where did you come from? If coming here was right, then where were you before?"

"I came from where I belonged, and I was where it was right. Now, I am here where it is still right."

What answers he has given. What little information. I'm scared to press for more, but he's been so polite. I would ask more questions if I knew how he'd react. But he knows too much, and he's given too little. I do not know him. When I watch him, he watches me. Wherever I go, he follows. Whenever I speak, he answers. Where is his agency? What is his intention? Did he even come here by choice?

"Please don't just speak to answer my questions. I want the truth, not just an answer."

"Everything I say is only the truth – there are no lies for me to tell. I can speak as you wish and answer your questions, but the words I use do not give answers their truth."

"Then tell me, please, why are you here? I only want to know what your purpose is."

"My purpose here is to live. And I live here because it's right."

So he says he lives here now. Maybe I made a mistake. Or was this his intention: for me to open the door? Does he follow me and speak to me in the hopes of stealing my life?

"You can't keep telling me that everything you do, you do because it's right. How can you even know what is right and what is wrong?"

"I know because I follow my heart. And my heart has told me right from wrong."

"Why should I trust you?"

"Because a heart wishes for only compassion."

In all the time I've known him, this is the most he has shared. And it explains nothing other than that he believes in his heart. I walked near to him. He wouldn't hold my gaze.

"Why do you follow me, and why don't you speak?"

Saying this, I grew angry. I let him into my life, and all he does is watch from the side. If he wishes to take part, he needs only to speak. I never before cared, but now I'm alone. Only now I felt he never cared: what compassion has he ever shown me?

"I follow you because I must. I do not speak because I can't. But together, we make a whole. Even if our selves are broken."

Now he calls me broken? I felt my rage, my inner anguish, all the emotion I dared not express. But he had done nothing. I couldn't yell. My anger could not surface. So I stilled my mind and grit my teeth.

"How long have you been here? You never even tried. I've lived my whole life since you arrived, and I've never asked you to speak. But you were always there. You have always watched. You know who I am, and you know how I feel. All I'm asking is for answers. Or at least for you to care."

He stood up and came closer – closer than he ever came before. He put his hand on my shoulder and looked into my eyes. The tears that welled took me by surprise.

"I have been here since you forced me out. There is nothing more that I can do. I can only listen to my heart and tell you what it says. But I have not the means to think. And you have not the means to feel. So we try our best."

"What *we* do you mean? It's only been just me. While you sat from afar, living through my life."

A part of me blamed him for all of my pain. He watched me live and never spoke. And his answers are all the same. In anything I ever asked, he simply said to do what's right. Now he has come closer, and now he has spoken more than ever. I blame him for waiting until this day. That all this time, he's always known. So came my anger and bottled up rage. So came the tears that I hid all these years. And he did not move.

"I understand what it is you feel – these feelings that you've never known. But you are the one who came to me. Even if you left me in the distance, I tried my best to understand. I can only answer the questions you ask. And how I've longed to speak my mind even if impossible.

"But now you come to me in need – for the first time in our life. I have spent my life alone. You felt you did not need me. Now, we are here. We can live the life you dream."

As he spoke, I saw the truth – my life flashing before my eyes. I felt the force of his pain where my heart once lied. Before I tore it out. So I took a step away. His hand pulled away. His expression became defeat. Quickly, the pain was gone. With it went my anger. I wiped away my tears.

"Why do you speak like you've been hurt? Like I did anything to you? I never wanted to get close to you because you never took interest in me. Don't tell me that you're lonely. You were there with my friends. It's only now that they're gone that *I* get to be lonely."

He stepped towards me. I stepped back. He stopped and went back to his seat.

"My heart told me it was the right thing to do. All I am capable of doing is listening."

"I don't understand. You say you can only answer. You say you can only listen. You say you cannot think. You tell me what you feel only now for the first time ever... Why?"

"You came close to me today. So I listened to you and spoke from my heart. It said it was the right thing to do."

Back to his old ways. I almost felt sorry, like I pulled back his heart to reveal his soul, only to force him to shut it away. But I did not feel. I did not feel anything except alone. Never before have I felt so empty. I stood there, by the door. I would leave and go to my friends – let them fill the void – but they are gone; I never felt the need to follow. So there's no life left for him to watch. And there's nobody else for me to know. So I went and sat beside him.

And as I did, I felt his pain. It filled my empty heart and soul. My pain became anger and anger, sorrow. We looked into each other's eyes, and I felt he knew my thoughts.

"I'm sorry that I did this. I didn't know it was wrong."

"And I am sorry too. I never could speak."

Bearing the weight of my heavy heart, I stood up. Though I was now alone, at least I finally understood. The right thing to do is to know the stranger in my chest. He knew so much about me, but about him, I never thought to ask.

Crawling Inside

What is it beneath my skin, crawling all around? The itching, twitching, deep within, whispering without sound. I watch it writhing, masses thriving, growing bigger day by day. But when I go outside, the masses run and hide, though I still feel them so deep within.

It's a pit in my stomach, churning around. The blood in my veins rings with the sound. I hear it in my ears, when silence closes in. The wriggling from inside sends echoes through my skin.

I want to go outside. I want to make it stop. But there's nothing to do, and there's nowhere to go. I've come to a place where there's nobody to know. I've been left with my mind, letting the creatures hatch inside. Now they're spreading through my body, I feel them in my chest. The few people I know ask me how I am – all I can do is say I'm trying my best.

Little do they know I'm being eaten away. I don't know what they are, but they're crawling inside. They're drowning out the silence, the sounds of my thoughts. All I hear is ringing, and it's slowly taking shape. I worry that I feed them with my fear – the more I struggle, the more it sounds like screaming.

How did they get here, take root in my head? These creatures are poison, killing me from inside. I can't fight my own body, and they know my thoughts. The door is so close, but they send me reeling. Bouncing around like butterflies, I haven't the strength to stop them. I wish I was stronger just to open the door, but I reach out my hand and the masses attack. They don't cause me harm, but their presence is pain. So I stay alone, trying to keep them contained.

But once in a while, I muster the force to push through the agony for whatever it's worth. I'm greeted by silence, but here there's no peace. Outside, I'm surrounded by people without the slightest idea. They wouldn't know that they're looking at someone who's trying their hardest, that I'm trying to ignore the thought of the night when the creatures will return angry, ready to fight.

But if I make it outside, I can keep the creatures within. No more echoes from the wriggling underneath my skin. I can ignore their holds within my stomach. I can endure their wrath while I enjoy the day. Though I suffer the cost of human interaction –

when others ask how I am and I don't know what to say.

But I can smile and say that everything is alright. With the creatures at bay, I do feel delight. I feel powerful in knowing that I have control. No matter their efforts, it's never enough. This is my life, and I will live it in full. But there's no one here for me to know. When the day is over, back inside is the only place for me to go.

I close the door and there they are. Their bouncing turns to twisting, wrapping around my chest. Squirming through my skin, building up my rage – I can't enjoy my own company if these creatures know me better than myself. They've come into my life, this body that was mine. Now they're taking over, costing me my health. Inside and out, they leave their mark: scars meant for me, wounds only I can see.

Their nest is my head, and it's running out of room. How much longer will I last before all I know is this dread? And I've made them angry, they know I want them out. I feel them growing larger, I feel their weight when I breathe. How much more time before I lack the breath to tell them to leave?

And they hear these thoughts. They feed off my fear. I'm making them stronger by feeling their pain. The ringing in the silence has become their whispers. Hundreds of voices telling me what to do. When I think of the door, all I hear is their horde. They tell me not to go, that I'll be ignored. That I'm no longer human and there's no room left in the world. They tell me to listen, to stay and obey. They warn me not to go outside – if I do, I'll spread their hive. Who am I to doubt their plea? I wouldn't wish this curse on anybody else. I wouldn't wish to be the one who kills their humanity.

So I stay inside and lie in bed. I can't lift the world they've made in my head. I can't move my legs, their masses keep me still. At least in the darkness, I can dream – of faces and places I've sworn away; of a life to be lived without a door in my way. Such is the life I consigned to them. Their voices, no longer whispers, tell me of the beautiful things they have in store. If only I wait a little bit longer, while every day they grow a little bit stronger.

I don't know if I can take any more. I'm running out of tears. I feel them moving through my heart, feeding off my pain. I feel them planting roots within. Their nests are growing just the same. Only now the masses appear with twisted faces showing. I fear where my life is going.

And on that darkest night, I had a dream. It was unlike anything else I had seen. In it, I met a person who was not like the others. Unlike all of the people I have known. Unlike all of the faces my mind has shown. This was not just a person. This was someone who was human.

So we talked about what we had in common. And I gazed upon a smiling face, feeling at once like I had a place. My mind had created a kindred soul. Though our talk was short, for just a moment, my heart was full.

I awoke to the screaming of writhing beings, and soon my dread returned. As they indulged, they grew quiet while a thought formed in my head. I saw the face of the only human I have known, and I was sad to imagine this was only a dream. How far have I fallen if the only company I know is the perfect person trapped in a dream?

In my sorrow, the creatures thrived. But for once, I didn't mind. In my head, I held the picture. The perfect face I hoped to make familiar. I don't think they knew any different – the difference between sorrow and hope. That the tears I let fall were not in mourning. They were of my sadness that for once I found moving – that somewhere out there must be another human.

So I stood up. And I was brought to my knees. Wreathing, screaming, consumed by agony, my eyes gazed at the door. Their voices filled every crevice of my mind. Their squirming filled every inch of flesh they could find. I held the image firm, giving light in the darkness. I struggled and lurched, inching towards the door. Slowly the face I was so quick to love became twisted with pain. Then the twitching and writhing came – the creatures already made it inside.

So I struggled through the darkness, reaching for the door. The pain was unbearable, impossible to ignore. No longer did I know the face I had seen. But the feeling I had known had only grown.

I turned the handle and fell outside. A concerned face held out a hand. Though I no longer remembered the human, the feeling I felt grew only stronger. Perhaps this was the right time and place, my dream become reality. Whoever this stranger used to be, they are now my humanity.

Inside Out

"Hey," I called, "put down the knife!"

Leon slowly lowered his arm, knife in hand, sliding through Joey's chest. He looked at me with cheerful eyes, his grin from ear to ear.

"Sorry!" He laughed. "Can't help it," he said with a sly, guilty smile.

"Oh, don't worry about it," said Joey, clutching at his wounds.

"Come on," I grumbled. Couldn't they save it for later? I was wearing my nice shoes.

We walked on through the street, Leon juggling his blades. Each catch and throw opened new wounds. His tendons were wearing thin. Our trail of blood had doubled.

"Hey!" came a hoarse voice. A man stepped out from a doorway. His intestines in his hands. "Can you hold this for a minute?" He held them out to me.

I sighed and took hold. Joey and Leon rolled their eyes. The man rummaged around inside, finally pulling out his heart.

"There it is! I thought I lost it!" Tears streamed down his eyes. They sparkled with his joy. He let out a crazy holler, pulling his innards from my grasp. Organs in hand, he ran off, skipping, yelling, hollering.

"Hmmph," Joey made his displeasure known, "you know better than to enable those weirdos." The color had drained from his flesh.

"What am I supposed to do?" I asked. "I'm not in the mood for getting stabbed."

"Suit yourself," Leon replied with a smirk, his blades lodged in his hands.

We carried on until we arrived just in time for our reservation.

"Three o'clock for Sam," I told the hostess. Her cheeks bore her teeth.

"Right this way," she struggled to get out. I noticed how effective this was to smile.

We reached our table and settled in. Though my menu was splattered with blood.

"What are you guys getting?" I asked.

"I'm in the mood for something spicy," Joey said first. "Maybe I'll try the tacos."

"Do you even need to ask?" followed Leon. "Why else would you even come here?"

We chuckled at the truth. Leon wasn't wrong. He would have his favorite sandwich, same as always. Just like I would have my bread.

"I guess I really don't need to ask. But you could always try something new," I suggested.

"I'll try something new, if you do too." Leon grinned. A twisted grimace.

I shook my head and laughed. He knew me too well. I suppose we were the same – we always ordered the same.

Our waiter came, eyelids nailed open, piercing through his brow. A stream of dried blood gave color to his cheeks.

"What can I get for you today?" he inquired.

"I'll have the tacos," Joey went first, "and a water-glass, please."

"And I'll have the sandwich," Leon said in turn. "By the way, I love your nails. Never seen that before!"

"Thank you. They've been nice to have," the waiter replied with a smile before looking to me.

"Can I get the bread? And would it be possible to make it easy on the eyes?"

"Of course, not a problem. Tacos, sandwich, bread – easy on the eyes – and I'll be right back with the water-glass. Is there anything else?"

We looked at each other, then back at him.

"That's all. Thank you," I said, sliding over my menu. Joey and Leon made no move, so I gathered their menus and handed them over. My hands were smeared with blood.

"Were you flirting with the waiter?" I asked Leon.

He tilted his head to an unnatural degree, making his smile look like a frown: "Maybe. Don't you think he looks nice?"

"You can't just flirt with anybody. And the nails, really?" I said, giving him a disapproving look.

He twisted his head the other way to look at Joey. I glanced over too to find him face down, fast asleep.

"He's looking nice and pale," Leon commented, touching his hand to Joey's forehead. "Oh, he's burning up. Good thing he got the water."

Once again, I shook my head. Poor Joey certainly didn't want to be stabbed. We were supposed to be enjoying a meal.

Just in time, the waiter came. He had the bowl of water and the glass.

"Here you are," he placed it by Joey, hesitating for a moment. "Does he need a hand?" he asked.

"I think so. Leon, here, just couldn't help himself," I answered. Leon's cheeks flushed.

"Happens all the time," said the waiter, winking at Leon as he lifted up Joey's head, quickly bringing it down on the table.

Joey instantly sat up, looking around. His eyes recognized us, one at a time, then he realized the waiter was watching him.

"Ah, sorry!" Joey said. He blushed in embarrassment at the waiter's sympathetic smile as he left. Joey shot Leon a glare.

"Whoops," said Leon with a shrug.

Joey picked up the glass and pulled the bowl in front of him. He crushed the glass in his hands, keeping the pieces small. There wasn't too much blood. He stirred the water, suspending the shards, and took his first sip.

"Perfect," he said, crunching on glass.

I wanted to comment, but held my tongue. I didn't approve of his drink, especially not after losing so much blood. But it was his favorite. Just like I didn't approve of Leon's favorite sandwich. I liked to keep my teeth in check.

"So, how was your date?" Leon asked me before the silence lasted long.

"Ooh, please do tell," Joey echoed his grin.

"It wasn't really a date," I said. "And she was rather strange."

"Strange how?" Joey asked, both of them leaning in.

"Well, she just didn't have any scars. And her knife didn't have a handle, so she asked for a different one."

Leon's eyes went wide. I could see him processing.

"Sounds like someone I know," Joey said, looking at me with an eyebrow raised.

"What?" I asked.

"Are you, of all people, complaining about that?" he replied.

"I'm not—"

"Oh, those are the crazy ones, aren't they," Leon interrupted. His twisted grin returned. "It's what you don't see you need to be careful of."

It was my turn to blush. It wasn't like that. I shouldn't have said anything.

"She was nice, though," was all I said. They exchanged looks.

"Did your knife have a handle?" Joey asked.

"No."

"And did you ask for one?" Leon pressed.

"I didn't want to be rude, but I didn't know she would ask."

They laughed. I didn't say anything else until the waiter arrived.

"Alright, here are the tacos," he said, picking up Joey's empty bowl, replacing them with his plate.

"And the bread." He sat my bowl in front of me. It was very easy on the eyes. Exactly as I had asked.

"And now..." He knelt by his cart as Leon watched on with excitement. He looked back at Leon, exchanging a smile, before setting the sandwich tray on top. It looked like a good sandwich. They changed the bread since we were here last.

He lathered his hands with the sauce. Leon was on the edge of his seat. The waiter picked up the bread and turned around, his fist up in the air. He struck Leon square in the mouth, then turned to grab the lettuce. Again, he struck, harder than before. The sauce was turning red. Once more, now with bacon. And again and again until the sandwich was made. Leon looked as though he'd pass out from the excitement.

"Hope you enjoy!" The waiter left us once more.

"Did you see his form!" Leon exclaimed with the brightest-red smile. "I think he even added extra just for me!"

I sighed while Leon wiped his face with the bread. What's the point of a sandwich you assemble yourself? These restaurants and their gimmicks.

I started picking through my bread. They used the nicest beef. But I could never bring myself to eat the eyes, and asking them to leave them out would be rude.

We ate in silence until we all finished. The waiter returned to clear the dishes.

"Anything else before the bill?" he asked us.

"That's all, thank you," I said before the others had a chance to speak. But that didn't work.

"Yes, actually," Leon said, pulling a blade from his hand. "Could I get your number?" He offered it to the waiter.

Without a word, the waiter took it, carving numbers into Leon's flesh; then he disappeared, brought out the bill, and left us to ourselves.

There wasn't anything I wanted to say. Thankfully, Joey finally finished pulling the staples out of his mouth.

"Nice one," he said with a chuckle, standing up to leave.

We took the short path, though they hadn't cleared the corpses in a very long while – the smell of decay was quite intense. We remained rather quiet. I just watched those crazy people, rummaging through their chests, crying tears of joy.

I thought back to my date, the girl I didn't know. It wasn't much, but Joey was right. Maybe I'm a weird one too. I looked down at my hands, still stained with blood, and the splatter on my shirt. From the corner of my eye, I looked at Leon; the way he wore his bruised and bloody face; the twisting of his neck; his bleeding arm. I glanced at Joey; pale as a ghost; lips rife with holes and splinters; the way he stumbled over the rotting bodies.

We soon parted ways, and I was finally free. Free to let my mind wander. Was it true, what Leon said? That those who don't bare their scars are the ones with things to hide? Was I wrong to judge her for requesting a handle, or should I have done the same?

And what even was it, in the first place, that has led us here? Why do they never clear the corpses? Why do those crazy people find so much joy in tearing out their insides? Why did Leon use his knife? Why did Joey get the water? Why didn't I? Why don't I understand? Is there something wrong with me?

I washed myself and looked in the mirror, my flesh mostly clean. I looked into my bloodshot eyes: today was not so good. I didn't enjoy my time. But is it wrong for me to say that I still thought it was fun? In the moment, anyway.

I could only look back. I saw the time we spent together. Joey. Leon. And everyone else. They lived a life they thought was normal. But I didn't. I never thought that it was right. That is why I hide my scars. And why I don't go chasing new ones. Is that what makes me crazy?

I couldn't stand to see my face any longer. I went over to the window, watching the pedestrians down below. How they walked, hand in hand, the occasional group of children. The businessmen in their suits. The workers in their uniforms. Old faces, here and there. Young faces, never far. Happy faces – everywhere. Everyone peacefully strolling about. Enjoying the sweet summer air.

The Cage of Birds

I grew up in a cage. Me and all my friends. We probably wouldn't be friends if not for the cage. But the cage was not a blessing. Nor were our wings. We were born to fly. We were different. We were special. And the others didn't like that. We were taken at birth as was the custom. We were born with wings, so we belonged in The Cage of Birds.

It was important that we were taken so young, before we learned to fly. As such, our wings didn't mean anything to us. They were only a mark of shame – what made us different – what made others mock us and abuse us. Many times we discussed our wishes to have been born like everyone else.

And it wasn't just a cage. It was a prison. They treated us "humanely" because we were still human. But we were no different from animals. What standards they had were never upheld. Nobody cared what actually happened to us. I think there was jealousy. Many of us agreed on that. They wanted our wings. They wanted to fly. But we were the special ones, so they turned our blessing into a curse.

Much of my life was a blur. Every day was structured and often exactly the same as the last. It was all we ever knew. But every day, we had time together. In our stolen lives, this time was the only time we could live. We didn't know much about the outside world. We heard about it. We saw it on occasion, not that we could understand it. Nevertheless, we knew what happened to us. Even if all we knew was suffering, we still knew we were suffering.

One of us flapped his wings once. He told us he was going to fly away. First, he had to learn how to fly. I was thirteen. He was twelve. We were children. I wanted him to succeed. But he tried flapping his wings, and the wardens saw – they were always watching. In all our time, he was the first to ever seriously try flying. The wardens pierced his wings as a warning and told us, all of us, to never try again.

That made him angry and bitter. Three years later, after years of slow and painful secrecy, he tried again. This time, he flew. That was how we learned what their weapons did. We learned our lesson.

Things only got worse after that. The outside world was growing. That meant each year brought new wings. With more people came new restrictions and new suffering. As my friends and I became who the young looked up to, we only cast our own pain down upon them. What hope the children had was lost to our faces. There was hope no longer.

But we could talk. And we did talk. By this point, we knew about the world. We knew all about the life that was taken from us. There wasn't a single soul in the cage who didn't despise their wings. We talked about other things, too. Like why we had wings in the first place. If we were out in the world, I imagine most would attribute them to their religion. There was no such thing in the cage. Instead, we had our own ideas.

Were we superior? That would explain the cage: that the others didn't like feeling inferior. Or being told what to do. That made us feel better. It made us feel better than them. But the joke was on us. We were the ones trapped in the cage. Their jealousy was nothing to our suffering.

Was it chance? Perhaps everyone was the same. Some are born male. Others are born female. We were born with wings. Same as the others. Maybe we weren't special. We didn't care. We didn't ask to be born. We didn't ask to be special. The others certainly didn't see it this way, however. Whatever feelings they had about us, they came from a place of hatred. The others aren't hated for the circumstances of their birth. That didn't feel fair.

129

Was it a higher power? We knew nothing of religion or gods. That didn't stop us from having our own ideas. We wondered whether someone or something made us this way. The most popular idea of all was that it was a test: how would the others treat us? Our belief was that everyone would be born with wings once the others learned to treat us like everyone else. Call it religion. Call it hope. It was the only thing we wanted.

Others, still, asked a different question. Was there a reason? We didn't need to be born with wings. So why were we? We didn't need to be ourselves. We could just as easily have been born as anybody else. So why did we see the world through our eyes – with wings? Of all the people we could have been. Of all the circumstances of our birth. Of all the times and places we could have been ourselves. Why us? Why there? Why then? It could only make sense if there was a reason. If our lives served some kind of purpose. If all our pain and our suffering was for some greater cause – something greater than ourselves that we could never understand. But this wasn't a very popular idea. Because it made us responsible for who we were and what we did with our excuse of a life. And that wasn't fair.

Whatever the reason, though, it didn't matter. The others had problems of their own. There was always fighting – domestic and otherwise. We saw the impact in our own lives. From food shortages to disappearing staff, we knew the cage wouldn't last. One of us would fail: us or the cage. The biggest tell was the number of young brought in. Each year fewer than the last. Until they stopped coming. Then the staff stopped coming. Then we were free.

The world was different from what little we had seen. Everyone wore sad, twisted faces. They still looked at us with anger and resentment. We were still treated like animals. But at least we were free. I had my friends. Others went their own way. We spent years trying to make sense of where we were and how to live.

Regardless of the circumstances – how we were raised and how we escaped – we knew only one thing, all of us. Caged birds don't fly. And they don't need wings. There was no reason to. Nobody wanted to. We still had wings, but they had been clipped. In my life, I only ever saw one of us fly. He found the freedom he sought. But it cost him everything.

Outside of the cage, I think everything was worse. We weren't the same without our shared experience. We didn't know what to think or feel without sharing our thoughts, together. We didn't know how to live without being told what to do. We didn't know how to be free after a lifetime in a cage. That made everyone miserable. Because the cage gave us a reason to live: to escape.

I watched the others crumble. One by one. Not everyone was so bad. But those were the exceptions. We spent our lives wondering why we had wings. Now I watch the others ask different questions. The few friends I have left ask if we would have been better off to stay in the cage. I wonder the same. The only question that isn't asked is why caged birds don't fly – not even when they're free.

Dark Compass

I'm lost in the dark left with only my compass. I can see what's close by, but there's not much to see. Anything beyond is lost in the dark.

My compass points me in one direction, but so often I come across forks in the road. They branch in all directions, I can't see where they go. The compass points me forward, but I have no choice. I must decide where to go off in the unknown.

I would say that I know what it is that I'm doing. I wish I could say that I had a sense of direction. But I have never turned around. I don't know how far I have come. Or if I've gone anywhere at all. I'm scared to turn around, to go back where I came. The last thing I want is to get lost where I've passed.

Not knowing where I am isn't always so bad. The path forward is anywhere with my compass in hand.

I don't need to know where I've already been. I don't need to know what I'm looking for in the end. Being lost and alone with nothing to own gives each step a sense of purpose and adventure. I follow the twisting, branching path, and what joy I feel when I step in the direction the compass points.

I've searched like this for many years, though there's nothing that I've found. Instead the closing darkness makes me see things quite profound. How long have I been here, being on my own? However long I've been lost and alone has shown me that I am my own home. Wherever I am or whatever I'm doing, the only person to go with me is whatever I am and whoever I might be.

So have I learned to be at peace with circumstance, for I did not ask for this endless task. For how long did I cry, screaming for help? How many times did I give up all of my hope? But here I am, me alone. With winding paths and a compass to hold, my feet carry me on to my meaning in life. I don't stray from the path, and I have no reason to go back. So onward I go, deep in the unknown.

Perhaps the greatest bitter truth, shown brightest in the great expansive darkness, is that my feet which carry me on are the very ones that brought this on. I made choices so naïve. I followed my heart to my darkest eve. I made plans, had hopes and dreams. But

I didn't know which way to go. So I put my heart into my compass. So I ventured off into the night.

At first it was easy, only one path to follow. The darkness was there, but I did not wallow. The compass agreed, so I went without worry. For days I went on until the path split in two. The compass pointed on, but the paths disagreed. This was the first time I felt I didn't have what I need. This was the first time I felt determined to leave. Not the way that I came, but to where I was going. So I chose the right path and refused to start slowing. The turns I took were quick and short. Day by day the compass inched closer. Until finally, at last, my direction agreed.

So on I went, never to stop. Until I came across a sea of countless ways to cross. Here I knew true despair. I came here in search of my truth, but so many ways to go was truly unfair. If only I could see what was on the horizon. To know what to do when I don't know where to go. My compass pointed back, but I followed this path forward. What else could I do but pick a path and start anew?

I picked myself up and picked a direction. The paths that I followed wound and curved. The compass pointed in circles. Branches branched, splitting my hope. I was alone, not knowing where to go, chasing hopes and dreams. The farther I went, the less sure everything seemed.

This was when I made this my journey: to escape from this place no matter the cost. The person I was had already been lost, but now was my chance to be reborn as I must.

So on I went, into the dark, never giving up. I don't know where I am or where I am going. Or who I am or what I lost. But I see light at the end of the tunnel. How long I was here, I will never know. The light that shines is such a beautiful sight. Though I had determination, I never found hope. But after all of this time, seeing light fills me with peace.

I watch and stare as it trickles down, shining light onto the path. And in the distance, so far away, I see beyond the horizon. Way out there is a shifting sea – a sea of branching paths. They twist and turn in every way, the ground spins in circles. Spinning and churning, creating something new – paths splitting and spinning into place. No sense of direction, just circles: a maze.

I really don't know what to say other than I'm lost here in the dark. I can see what's close by, but there's not much to see. Anything beyond, I wish I didn't know.

The compass points me in one direction, but the direction is not a place. I am lost and alone with nothing but my compass. In it, I put my heart as I followed my dreams. With it, I wandered deep into the dark. Never did I imagine that when I saw the light, it would reveal to me the truth that it was all a pitiless plight.

What, then, did I learn? Who, then, did I become? What, then, was the point? What is the outcome? I'm standing here, spinning in circles. I wandered on, facing my fears. I picked myself up, became someone new. I braved the unknown, learning to live life alone. I thought that in myself, I learned how to make a home. But it was all for nothing. So the light has shown.

Now with direction, I go back the way I came. I don't bother with the paths, I'm done playing their game. After however long I've been gone, I stand here in the day. The sun is shining down, revealing life all around. But I no longer find this very profound. Nor seeing the others, their smiling faces spewing joyful sound.

What was the cost of learning who I am? Who did I become in the sunless land? I made a home inside myself. I put everything aside to follow my heart. The only place it took me was into the dark.

Was I wrong to have hopes and beautiful dreams? Was I wrong to believe that I could be happy? Was I wrong to endure endless suffering, thinking pain would strengthen me and determination would carry me?

Now when I see the world outside, the sun beats down on darkness. I spent my days trying to break through, but it was only when I finally left that I lost sight of the horizon. When at last I can see where my paths lead, I no longer have a heart with which to lead.

Perhaps I found meaning in my suffering and built my character to endure. I thought what I did was right. I didn't know life could play a game. Out there, each day was different. Now, each day is just the same. So I sit and watch the others walk. They follow their chosen paths. And I look down and see my compass. I watch it spin in circles as I hold it to my chest – the only thing left with any meaning – as I think of those I left behind and of my life that was perfectly fine; if only I had known.

Me, Myself, and I

I met Myself at a lounge. Me was also there, they had arrived before I did. They chose a small table in the back – one with a beautiful view. As I walked over, I couldn't help but notice. It was a marvelous day. Me and Myself shared joyous expressions as I stared, watching the worlds drifting by in the vast cosmic expanse. All the souls and all the people. Everything that ever is, all gliding past the window.

"Perfect, isn't it?" asked Myself.

"I've never seen anything like it," I said in awe.

"Yes. What an incredible feeling," said Me, also watching the display.

I sat down across from them. We had difficulty focusing our attention on one another. I was distracted by a galaxy composed of three perfect planes orbiting a massive black hole when Myself lowered the blinds.

"That should make things easier," chuckled Myself. "Now let's get down to business. You said you weren't happy?"

Me and I looked at each other, lips pursed. I was hoping Me would speak first. Me's gaze, and expression, didn't waver. Myself looked on with a sad compassion.

"That's right," I spoke up. "It's nothing against Me. I just don't know what to do. When you aren't around, everything falls apart."

"Have I not been around?" asked Myself. "Have you two not discussed this?"

Me and I looked at each other again, expressions unchanged.

"Talking hasn't been so easy," Me said at last. Me looked down at the table. "I think we're trying to ignore each other. Not on purpose, but because we've drifted apart and we're scared of what might happen if we get too close." Me's voice was distant. Hearing Me say that was painful, but I knew we both felt exactly the same. I decided to open up as well.

"It hurts too much – being near Me. It's easier when I'm on my own. But then I see Me talking to you, and that just makes things worse. I feel so alone, and I know that's ironic, but I can't bring myself to go near Me. I don't have it in me to reach out to you, either. And you and Me talk, but you never talk to me."

Myself leaned back, taking in our sorry sights.

"You never say anything," said Myself. "It saddens me when I don't hear from you, but I tried before. It hurts me when I'm the only one who ever wants to meet."

"I know," I said. "I guess it's not just Me. I want to be around both of you, but I also don't want to do anything at all... even though I do. I want to reach out to you, both of you, but I don't know how. So I don't."

"And I'm scared of what I'll feel if I reach out to you," said Me. "That's why I talk to Myself."

"So what can we do about this?" I asked Myself. "Can we ever go back to the way things were?"

Myself let silence come over us. Me and I held our heads low in the heavy atmosphere. I wanted to open the window and lose myself in all the sights. I wanted to beg Myself to speak up – to tell me what I needed to do. I wanted to tell Me how sorry I was. I wanted to want to do anything at all.

"And what were things like before?" Myself asked after what felt like a lifetime.

"Everything was easy," I said after contemplating for a moment. "I just did whatever I wanted. I didn't think about it, and I was happy. I would talk to Me about anything and everything. You were never far, always offering your help. You directed and guided us whenever we asked. Me and I didn't need too much, though. Everything was so simple.

"Words came out without any thought. The right words – what I wanted to say. Feelings came without any pain. There was nothing for Me to complain about. When there was, it felt like the end of the world. But I was there to accompany Me through it. And it always went away quickly. Painlessly.

"If I wanted to talk about something, I met with you. Sometimes it was serious. Often it wasn't. You always listened, and I enjoyed listening to whatever you had to say. And I listened to what you told me to do. And I wanted to do it. And I wanted to do anything at all."

"So what happened?" asked Myself. "What made you change?"

"I thought it wasn't enough," I answered. I was surprised how quickly I knew what to say; all the realization came flooding in. "I saw everyone else and everything they had. I saw their lives and their dreams and their aspirations. And I saw what they were doing about it. All I ever knew was you and Me. I never thought about anything more. So I tried to change things, to be happy and motivated like them. But I didn't know how. I failed, so I thought it was too late.

"That's what happened: I saw too much in the process. But I didn't see myself. Until it *was* too late. Now I don't know who I am. And I have nothing. I left you and Me behind. Now I understand what I should have done – how important you both are. And now it's too late.

"I don't want to go back because only now do I understand. But I don't want to stay here because all I feel is regret. I don't even know who I want to be. Or what I want. It broke me to see you, together, like those others... without me."

"Then you *did* reach out," said Myself gently.

"To both of us," added Me.

"I did," I said. "Only because I didn't know what else to do."

"Isn't that the point?" asked Myself. "We only exist for each other. Because we are the only thing we will ever have. You'll never be happy without us. And we'll never be happy without you."

"And it's not too late," said Me. "Now that you've been gone, I think we'll grow to appreciate each other all the more."

"So what do I do?" I asked them both.

"You start by asking what *we* should do," Myself laughed, always knowing what to say. That brought a smile to our faces.

"Okay. What do *we* do?" I said, already feeling better.

"You said you have a lot of regrets because only now do you know what you should have done, right?" questioned Me.

"Yes, that's right," I answered.

"Then that's what we do. What we should have done. Just starting today," said Me.

I had been crying. There were tears in Me's eyes as well. Myself was Myself's usual calm and collected self – always with eyes full of compassion. I got up and hugged them both. I felt a sense of peace at knowing how to move forward.

So I raised the blinds. First, I saw my reflection. My red eyes and streaked cheeks. My face, a little more familiar. Then the people – all the lost souls. People whose journeys I will never know. Each one of them, an entire world waiting to be understood.

The Cost of Life

Every morning, I eat alone, looking out the window, gazing at the stars. Wherever I am – whatever I'm feeling – the stars fill me with hope. They give me hope for the future, knowing that somewhere, so unfathomably far away, must be someone else – or something else. Maybe a long-forgotten mining colony left to fend for themselves. Maybe the smallest of research stations, isolated, lost to the world. Maybe some undiscovered alien race, looking up in my direction, wondering if they, too, are alone.

Sometimes, the quiet gets to me. Sometimes, I long to speak to my family; my friends; my crew. Anyone at all. I want to hear their voices. I want to hear them speak – to hear anything real. But all I have are messages. Recordings of the past. Broken records. I long for something new.

I had an assistant. My second-in-command. It helped me through the darkest times. But I can only listen to a robot for so long. At least it kept me company. But I enjoyed shutting it off. Some part of me still blames it for sending everyone away. I trusted it. They trusted me. There wasn't anything else I could do. I didn't like the idea. It was the only idea. I listened to a machine.

After they left, the temperature dropped. Life support was failing. So I turned off the computer – sent the power to the heat. I needed to, I tell myself. That was my loneliest day. Food, water, air, and heat. I have nothing that I need.

Still, I try to hold myself together. Every once in a while, I send a message back home. They'll never receive it. I tell myself I tried. It makes me feel a little less alone. I started writing letters, too. Even if they'll never leave my side. I find peace in knowing they have a chance of being read – some day.

In the afternoon, I like to read. Most books are still on the computer. But I have enough with me. I enjoy the stories of space exploration – the early days. Of people getting stranded in their ships. On other planets. On remote stations. I enjoy reading about the efforts of humanity – turning tragedy into a cause – bringing humans together. "Leave no man behind," they said. And no man ever was.

To think that people ever cared about anyone but themselves. The age of exploration: the days when our world left the earth. It was the first time anyone bothered to ask if life had any purpose. Land didn't matter. Money didn't matter. Power didn't matter. "There are planets made of gold," they said. The only thing that mattered was the awe in people's hearts. That they could see the stars and live on other planets. So everyone was rich: rich in opportunity. They banded together, sailed the sea above, and built resplendent civilizations. Then someone got greedy: "*My* planets of gold." Of course, I can never know which stories are really true. And I can't say that I really care.

The only truth I know is that I'm alone. No one will come looking for me. I will always be alone. All those years ago, I would have been a hero. Now I'm just another lost soul, drifting through the stars. I'm here, alone, with an entire city to call mine. What a reward I could offer for someone to help. I imagine what would have happened if the shuttle really made it. If there were anywhere to go. Would I have made someone rich? Would I be a hero?

The shuttle. I find it all ironic. What is the cost of life? Is mine worth more than theirs? Did they even need to go? I have so many questions. I'll be long dead before I have any answers. In any case, I know that *I* wasn't the one shown mercy.

I often walk around in the evenings. I must wear a suit and pack oxygen. It's heavy. It's uncomfortable. But I need a reason to keep going. I walk and walk down the endless rows, fields of the living dead. They have no names. I thought of naming them. But I can't bear the thought that they'll never live to know.

I wonder, though, if they could one day learn of their origin, would they feel the same sense of guilt? Would they know or understand the cost of their life? Would they long for a home, for loved ones never had? As I wander the endless halls, I wonder what will become of them. Maybe, one day, they'll know love. Maybe they'll be happy. Maybe they'll be grateful for the sacrifices made in their name. Or so I tell myself. Anything so I don't give up. Anything to keep life support on. Because everyday is yesterday. I don't have a tomorrow. But they do. I hope they do. I want to hope, even if I'll never see it. So I think of them as my children. I live to give them life. So I tell myself.

I don't sleep at night. I can't stand turning off the lights. What dreams I have are of hundreds of thousands of cries for help, begging me to end it all. They call my name. They call me "father." They beg me to show them mercy.

I dream of the broken earth. It's halves swallowed by the sun. I dream of humanity's reach. So far apart – yet so connected – yet never far enough. I dream of the fires in the skies. Planets cracking. Stars exploding. I dream of nebulas of human remains. I dream of places. I dream of faces. I dream such terrible dreams.

But my dreams have no power over me. When I turn off the lights, I am brought to my knees by the ghosts of those who trusted me. My friends. My family. My crew. They watch me from the shadows. Purple faces. Blood-red eyes. Burnt flesh. Their eyes pierce my heart. Their expressions merely asking "why?" Their mouths open in violent screams. When I close my eyes, I see the shuttle. I hear myself telling them it's safe. I feel myself embracing my children. My voice echoes through my mind: "Come back with help." It's too much to bear. When I open my eyes, they surround me. "I showed you mercy," I shout at them. I can't meet their questioning stares. My wife grabs my shoulders: "Mercy isn't yours to give."

I try to run, but they're always there. I try to hide, but there's nowhere left. They stand there. Surrounding me. Watching me. "What life will those children have?" they plead. "The same as yours?" they ask, parting to let me see. They stand there, the two of

149

them, such anger in their eyes. "You did this to us, father," they shout. Their twisted, broken limbs. "It was the only way," I yell. "I did it for our future," I shout. "*Our* future?" questions my wife, the rage in her voice. "*You* made certain," she chokes, her voice violently shaking, "that there's no future to be had." I cry. I weep. I mourn.

I Hope You're Happy

I followed your instructions. I hope that makes you happy. You were getting quite concerned. You told me how you felt. You said there was much for me to do. It wasn't an easy choice. All the things I had to sacrifice. But you said I needed to. You said it would make me happy.

I knew what I wanted to do. But you told me it was wrong. You said I never could. And that if I did, I would fail. You said I wasn't normal. And everyone else agreed. You gave them all instructions, too. They followed them. They were happy. I watched them grow happy all around me. But I wasn't happy. You said it was my fault.

I didn't want to listen. But there was nothing else for me to do. I wasn't happy. Did I have a choice? You laid it all out before me. All so crystal clear. Step by step, you paved the way. You told me everything to do. I asked you a few questions. First you had compassion. You said it was alright, that I would soon understand. You showed me what you meant. You explained the instructions. And I started following. But it didn't work.

So I came back to you. I didn't get very far. You were upset – mad that I didn't keep going. "How foolish could you be?" is what you exclaimed when I told you it didn't feel right. "Do you not see what comes next?" You pointed at the list. I gave in. I figured I might as well try. You were right, after all, that I could have gotten started. Everyone else already had. I guessed it was just me.

Then it became difficult. I wasn't only unhappy. I dreaded each day because I couldn't keep up. The tasks you laid out were draining my soul. It wasn't good. It wasn't right. So I came back. I asked you for help.

"I don't think this is working." That's what I said. You laughed at me, and unfolded the list. "Look at where you are. You've only just begun. And you're already so far behind. That's what's going wrong. Look at everybody else. Can't you see how happy they are? If anything is wrong, then it is wrong with you." That was your answer. You made me cry.

You weren't wrong, though. I saw that it worked. Everyone else was following along. They didn't ask questions. And they succeeded. They were all so happy. So if anything was wrong, then it was me. Nothing else made sense. I didn't see anything bad. Your instructions were long, but they made perfect sense. Others complained, and then they continued. I was going slow. Maybe I should have tried to catch up.

So I went faster. It actually worked. With so much to do, there was no time to complain. By filling the time, there was no reason to be sad. And each step that I took was a step in the right direction. By the time I finished, I could only be happy. That was how it worked. I saw it in everybody else. It was exactly as you said.

Everyone I met pointed to the person ahead. "I can't wait for that one!" they would tell me. They had a sparkle in their eyes. And radiant smiles. At first, I was apprehensive. "I don't know," I would reply, "it seems so far away." But everyone was happy to help. They knew I was behind – because I was older. Maybe not by much, but it doesn't take much being young.

Their optimism spread. I was busy. Busy and looking forward to the future. You were proud. "Now don't you see?" you asked me. "This is how it works. You pick a direction – forward – and you go. And you don't stop until you reach the end!" This is what the others told me, too. I felt hopeful. "I think I understand," I told you, "I think I know how to be happy."

Though I wasn't happy yet. There was still more to do. So with everyone else, I kept on my way. Step after step, all following instructions, we made our way to the end. Year after year, we struggled together. Crossing an item off the list was cause for celebration. And always in front were those ahead – how we longed to follow in their footsteps.

Once, I got tired. I decided to rest. I paused for only a moment, but that was all it took. My companions moved on. New faces passed by. I lost sight of those I was following. As soon as I stopped, I began to feel. It was that sadness – that longing – from so long ago. My will to continue vanished. What was the point? What even was there at the end? I'd never thought to ask.

"Hey!" I called to the passersby. "What are we working towards at the end?" They gave me blank stares. "Happiness," said some. "Purpose," said others. But all of them said one thing the same: "Don't ask me, just look ahead. We'll see the end in only a few more steps! The final instructions!"

I needed your reassurance. "Oh, you naïve fool. You were so close to the end! Don't waste your time on me. Get moving!" You had little else to say. You wouldn't let me talk. But I agreed. There was little time to waste – not after I had wasted so much already. And I was close. So I picked myself up and went on to the end.

Step by step, only a little more slowly, I made my way. Those around me stared in awe: the end. We could see it. There were a lot of people. There seemed to be a fuss. Or was it excitement? We were too far to tell. We continued on until we completed your instructions.

"That's it?" they were shouting. "What happens next?" There they were: those who had gone on ahead. I walked with them once. Then I admired them from afar. Now we stood together. "What's going on?" I asked them. "This is it. There's nothing else to do. There is nothing else," they answered. "You say that like you're disappointed," I commented. "I thought this would make me happy," they replied.

That was when I understood. I understood it all. I followed your instructions. All the way to the end. And that was the end. The end of me. You wasted my life. There is nothing left. You said I'd be happy. Like everybody else. But you're the one smiling. You're laughing at me – and everybody else. To you, this was a game. You set us all up. You tricked us into believing that instructions could be followed.

We were all the same. Every single one of us. I wasn't so different. I simply dared to ask. I wasn't a fool. I wasn't naïve. I was brave. Going fast was only a distraction. You didn't want us to feel. But I felt because I went slow. You didn't like that. So you gave me your attention. You twisted my pain. You turned it on me. But you caused it. And you hid it. You lied too well. You tricked me.

I've caught up to the others. We're all here at the end. We speak to each other, sharing our stories. And they all say the same: "I thought you were happy." What were you thinking you would accomplish? I should have known when I asked you questions. If you wanted to help, you would have understood. Instead you hurt me. You told me I was wrong. I guess you've succeeded. Now you're the last man alive. There's nobody else. Nothing else to be had. You've acquired the world. And you're the only one in it.

Cracked Skies

"Did you get Bjorn's message last week?" Anna asked.

"I haven't checked." My heart skipped a beat. "I really need to do that!"

If I didn't get back to Bjorn in time, he would be devastated. I imagined him, the next time we met, giving me his disapproving look: "So you missed it. *Again*," he would say with that infuriating tone.

"Yes, you did. You needed to *last week*." Anna let out a disapproving noise of her own. There was no escape. This would be a long walk.

"I'm sorry! It just slipped my mind. I'll do it tomorrow. I promise." I tried to sound convincing – to convince myself. I pulled out my phone while Anna watched me set a reminder. At least it was a start.

I bumped – head first – into a stranger.

"Sorry!" I said, though he should have apologized. He stopped, for no reason, right in front of me... everyone had stopped. They were all looking up. Even Anna.

I looked up. I saw the sun – a massive, orange ball – slowly growing bigger and bigger while the color grew into a deeper and deeper orange. After only a few seconds, it was too bright to look at. Everyone shielded their eyes. What must have been shock soon turned to panic. People hunched over, screaming. The heat was growing, too. What felt like warm sunshine at first soon grew to a burning sensation.

"We need to go," Anna said, grabbing my arm.

Like everyone else, we ran. Through the screaming. Everyone with their arms in front of their eyes. I heard what most of them were saying: "I can't see!" they were calling out; "My eyes!"

Anna guided me into the subway. I don't know what I would have done without her.

"Are you okay?" she asked.

"I think so, are you?" I asked in return.

"*I'm* okay. But what in the world is going on?" she frantically questioned.

I looked up the stairs, up to the distant entrance. Blinding light shone down on us. With it, heat like I'd never felt before. I didn't reply to Anna. She watched with me. Everyone else, below the surface, watched as

158

the ball of fire grew and grew. We watched until there was nothing left. Of us. Or the earth.

"Setting a reminder isn't going to get it done," Anna scolded me.

I sighed as we carried on. There was no point in arguing with her. It was no secret that I would rather procrastinate. I didn't feel like talking as we went down into the subway, making the slow and agonizing journey to the office.

And upon our arrival, there he was. Bjorn. He didn't see me, though. I grabbed Anna's arm and pulled her with me to the side.

"Seriously?" she said in an angry whisper.

"What do I do?" I asked. "Can I just tell him I got caught up with something personal?"

"That's what you said last time." Anna rolled her eyes – and her head – pulling me over to him.

"Hey, Bjorn. I'd love to talk, but I've got work to do!" Anna smiled at him, gave my arm a very aggressive squeeze, and walked off.

"Hello," I said awkwardly. "I should go get started on that... thing you wanted me to do."

"Oh," he said, eyebrows raised, "that would be very helpful." At least he didn't give me the look. I hurried off to my desk.

I sat down, turned on my computer, and pulled up my email. Then it turned off. I was finally bringing myself to get some real work done. Frustrated, I tried turning it back on. Nothing happened. I groaned and crawled under the desk. All the cables were plugged in. Nothing was wrong that I could see.

Then I felt the ground start to rumble. It was an earthquake. I ran back to the lobby. Anna, Bjorn, and everyone else was there. All the lights were off. The power must have gone out.

"Come on," Anna called me over. "Let's get to the stairwell."

I took one step, then the building began swaying. I could feel it. The force knocked me to the ground. Everyone else was on the floor, crawling under the tables.

On my hands and knees, I made my way to Anna. The swaying grew worse and worse as a deep rumbling filled the air. The shaking became violent. Anna grabbed my hands. We just sat there, looking into each other's fear-filled eyes as the world shook.

The windows exploded. All of them. At once. A vehement shockwave tore through the building. It pushed me back, the force gluing my limbs to the wall behind me.

After only a few terrifying minutes, deafening silence filled the room. I pulled myself away from the wall. My body felt light. My head felt like it was going to explode. I couldn't control my movements. Everyone was muttering. Some were bleeding. Bjorn had pulled himself up with a door frame.

"Is everyone alright?" he called out. His voice wavered. I could barely hear him.

"No," came a quiet voice. A small group had gathered among the broken glass, looking off into the distance. All completely silent. We stumbled over to them, limbs flailing awkwardly like toddlers.

"My God," Anna whispered. No one else dared to speak.

Up in the sky, the black sky, was the earth. Half of the earth. And a glowing trail of fire. Below us were the ruins of the city. Twisted metal, demolished buildings, debris falling in slow motion.

Anna fell to the ground. I couldn't breathe. Darkness began closing around the corners of my vision.

I opened Bjorn's email. I probably should have done that last week, at a minimum. It was a simple task, too. A promotional flier for his upcoming event. It would probably take me a few days. I laughed to myself with that realization – I could have finished already. If I bothered to open the email.

So I got started. I worked late. I was probably half way through in only one day. I felt a sense of accomplishment as I shut off my computer and prepared to leave.

Anna walked by, saw me, and came back.

"You're still here?" she asked.

"I finished half of the flier!" I said proudly, putting on my coat.

"I'm impressed. You'll finish with whole days to spare at this point," she mocked.

"Have you gotten much done?" I asked her.

"Honestly," she paused for some time, "not really." She dropped her usually cheerful demeanor.

"Sorry to hear that. How about dinner?" I hoped spending some time together would bring both our moods up.

"Alright," she said after another pause, "but you're paying." We laughed and headed to The Twelve.

Walking in the evening was always depressing. All the vagrants were out and about, drug addicts laid out on the sidewalks. Shouting matches came from open windows. And everyone walked around with their heads down.

Anna was always the one who tried to maintain a good mood, but I didn't mind being the one every once in a while. It gave me a sense of purpose – being able to be there for her. Maybe that's how she did it, too. She knew the impact her smile would have on me and everyone else around her – something so simple.

"Are you alright?" I asked. We sat across from each other. I had to speak up. The bar was crowded.

"I don't know," she answered. "I can't help but feel like there's not enough time, and I'm wasting what little I have."

"Yeah." I didn't try to sound cheerful. "I understand."

We ordered and ate in silence. The mood spoke for itself. We weren't sad. Just empty. Unless that's what sadness is. But I think she enjoyed the time together as much as I did. It wasn't a happy dinner. But it was good to simply be with each other.

"Thanks," Anna said as we parted ways. "See you tomorrow."

"See you tomorrow." I gave her a sad smile. As she walked away, it started to rain. I hurried towards the subway.

With each step, the wind picked up. Within minutes, torrents fell from the sky. I watched the few people with umbrellas struggle to keep them open. A thin layer of water already filled the streets. I had to lean into the wind to keep moving forward.

But I couldn't. Not too far behind me was a rooftop lounge. I figured they were open. It sounded like a good place to hide away until the storm passed. Turning around, my feet were aided in rushing me inside. A number of others had the same idea. Not too many people for a Thursday night, though. For a lounge, it was empty.

With a glass of water, I sat by the window, looking down at the city. It was a lot more comfortable than the office. I relaxed and let my mind wander. There was a lot to think about. Too much. All the sad faces around me, all staring out at the rain, told the same story: too much on everyone's mind. The fact they were all here alone, like me, said a lot too.

The rain didn't stop. The rain never stopped. It got worse and worse. The wind only picked up speed. I watched cars drift below, carried away by the risen sea. I watched the smaller buildings wash away into nothing. I listened to the screams and cries from down below for days. For nights. It was always dark. Everyone in the lounge with me did the same. Some cried. Most simply watched and stared. I didn't even check my phone. I thought about Anna. I hoped she was alright. But it wouldn't make a difference.

The water rose. It kept rising. Until it began pouring into the lounge. There was nowhere to go. There was nothing to do. I sat as it poured over my legs. I drifted up and up, into the ceiling. I floated until I could float no more.

The next day, I finished the flier. Anna didn't come in – that was probably a good thing. She said she needed a day off to think, and I didn't mind spending the day without distraction. It felt good to get work done. It was good work, too. Bjorn would be happy – and hopefully proud. I certainly felt proud.

"Here's the flier." I handed him the first print. He took a minute, reading all the text, holding it up to different backgrounds. Holding it up to the light at different angles. Checking all the edges of every shape. Everything had to be perfect.

"I'm impressed," he said after the charade. "Looks like it's ready to go. One hundred thousand perfect replicas. Can you believe that?" He smiled at me.

"Not really, sir. It sounds like a dream!" It was true. I couldn't believe that my work was soon to be plastered all over the city – the entire city.

"Or a nightmare," he joked. He seemed happy. And I was free.

"Is there anything else you need from me before the event?" I asked.

"I don't think so. You're free to go and do whatever you want. I'll see you on Wednesday, then." His smile left as he said this. Mine did too. We looked at each other in silence. The same mood as The Twelve. There were no words to say. I went home.

On Sunday, I met with Anna. She was back to her cheerful self. I was in a similar mood. I'd spent the past day and a half admiring my work. It really was everywhere. Every billboard and every building.

"You've done a good job," she greeted.

"Well hello to you, too. But thanks. And thanks for getting me on it."

"It's not like it would have mattered one way or another," she said with a smile. Though her eyes didn't.

"I guess not. I can't believe it's just a few days away. I don't even know what to do. Or how to feel."

"Have you talked to your family and all your friends?" she asked.

"Of course. Everything is all set."

"Then I guess we just wait. And see how we feel." She smiled at me. This time with her eyes. I felt the faintest ember in my heart. Like everything was going to be just fine.

Wednesday came too quickly. I was ready though. Anna came by my place, and we headed to Bjorn's big event together. The streets were crowded. Bjorn reserved one of the rooftops for all of us. He said we deserved a good view for all our hard work. A sea of people poured out in every direction. Every building was crowded – most rooftops as well. I stood with Anna. The stage was right below us. I doubted most people could see anything from the streets.

First were the speeches. I didn't pay too much attention. I don't think anybody did. Then the music. Nothing special. Then Bjorn talked. He talked about how happy he was to see everyone there, together. He pointed up to us on the rooftop, asking everyone to give us a hand for helping put the event together. I'd never heard clapping like that before. And the cheering. It sounded like the earth being ripped in two. It was a good feeling.

Then the countdown started. Two hours. Bjorn had told us that was a good length. It was the perfect amount for everyone to think and reflect without growing anxious. He wasn't wrong. For two hours, the world was silent. For two hours, Anna and I held hands. Not one word was said. I don't think anyone said a word. Not one soul on the entire planet.

Then the sky grew dark. Then our worlds collided.

I Killed God

I sat at my bed, praying for mercy. I begged God for His forgiveness. For everything I have done. I didn't mean to. I didn't want to. It was all a big mistake.

"Please have mercy on my sins. Please have mercy on my sins..." I repeated, over and over again, rocking back and forth, tears streaming down my face.

I don't know how long I sat there. Maybe hours. Even days. I would never have stopped. I would have been happy to die there. But such is human nature: I was tired. I was hungry. I was thirsty. And I didn't want to die.

I'm sure I passed out at some point. All I remember is standing up and all my feelings disappeared. All of them. I wiped my tears and went downstairs. After some time, I went for a walk. There were no thoughts in my head. I didn't even feel the cold. Or the wind. Or the rain. I don't think I wore a coat.

It was early in the morning. Before the sun was up. I only remember because I walked until it was. I watched its light reach through the clouds. That was the only thought I had: *This could have been a sign.* But I knew it wasn't. God couldn't talk. He never did before. He never will. Nobody will ever get a sign.

The only signs I ever received were cruel with twisted humor. On my darkest night, I prayed for a sign. I begged for mercy. To give me a chance. To let me live. To let me be happy.

"Please just give me a sign. Just show me that you're real. That this isn't all for nothing," I begged. "Tomorrow. That's all I need. Anything."

The following day, I got my sign. It couldn't have been more clear. I didn't even know that it was what I wanted. But I got a message, from a friend, saying exactly what I never knew I needed.

I thanked God for having mercy. For the first time in so very long, I was happy. I met my friend – that was the message – he had invited me on a trip. Out of the blue. On the day I asked to receive the sign. Because I was so alone.

He greeted me with kindness. He talked and filled the room. He was the first person I had seen in a rather long while. I didn't know what to say. Though he was happy to do the talking. But all I could do was watch, see the person I could never be.

The trip lasted for two days. The first we spent alone. Then he picked up his friend, a good man I'd never met. He joined us. And they talked. About things I didn't know. People. Places. Times. Events. They talked like best of friends. He changed, my friend, he'd come alive. The life I never knew. They were kind to me. They talked to me. I simply never knew what to say. So when the trip was finally over, I thanked him for the invitation and went on my own way.

I cursed God for his cruel joke. For making me think that was a sign. All He did was show me that I could not be happy. I never would. I never could. It simply wasn't in me. Those happy people, truly friends. Together being human. So what was I? Why can't I? Why can't I join their fun? I could have. If I tried. I could have tried to fit in. But I didn't want to. It wasn't me. So who am I if I'm not dead? I know that I'm not human.

A few days later, I had a dream. It stood out in some strange way. There wasn't much, but I met a stranger. I drove up into the clouds. That's where I met her. Her hair was recently shaved. She worked inside a ship, up there in the sky. A ship made of rope. But the inside was normal. And she was a researcher. What that meant, I didn't know. But the bond we formed, I did. It was a feeling, so surreal. That I could know a stranger. All we did was talk – all the things we had in common. She was like myself. And I liked her. It made me sad when I woke up.

"God, I'm sorry for what I've done. Please have mercy on my sins. I think I understand what you were trying to say. You wanted me to know all the things that I lack. So I can fix myself. And meet the person from my dream."

I prayed in earnest, though I was confused. What kind of dream would leave me feeling this way? And what did all the symbols mean? A few days later, I got my answer. Another invitation. Though I didn't know it at the time; I was just happy for a chance to get away. And maybe practice being human.

Nothing really happened. I can't say it was so fun. However, I made a friend. Or rather, met someone. Someone new. That was new. She was working on some research. Then we left. That was that. Then I got home. And I remembered. That this was from my dream.

Everything. All the symbols. I saw how they made sense. So I thanked God for having mercy and reached out to my new friend. We talked at first. It all made sense. This really was that person. And we met. And we talked. And then we met again. I couldn't believe what I was experiencing – that a dream could come true.

Then she went away. And that was the end. As quickly as it started. It made no sense. I didn't understand. Where did she even go? Was it all in my mind? Was it even real? Or was it me forcing my perfect story upon her?

"God," I begged, "what have you done? Are you trying to make me suffer? How could you make a dream come true, then take it all away? It wasn't a dream after all. You've made my life a nightmare."

He never answered. Not with words or a message. So when I saw the light reaching through those clouds, I was struck by their beauty. It could have been a message. Saying things would be alright. But I have learned that's not how God works.

I do try, though. I do my best. Without His helping hand. I worked my way up from the bottom. My hands did all the work. For all my prayers and all I've suffered, it was only ever me. I asked and prayed and did my best, but God was never kind, and neither was the world.

All I was left with were my memories. Of all the times God found humor in my prayers. It made me angry to think that He was in control. He did this to my life. Then He dares to mock me. Realizing this prompted my final prayer. There was only one thing I wanted God to know.

"God," I prayed, "if you're there. Why don't we have a talk? Just you and me. One-on-one. I want to know what you have planned."

It wasn't much, but it would do. I didn't care if He didn't answer. I didn't need Him, anyway. I wondered, though, if He'd be hurt. If I disappeared from His life. Just as He had taken so many away from mine and caused me so much hurt.

Then He appeared. In the night. He finally wished to talk.

"Why do you curse my name?" He called.

I got out of bed, confused. In the faint light of the moon, I saw Him. Behind the mirror. I went over and stared at Him, standing beside my reflection. It was me. Two of me. He had taken my form.

"Why do you look like me?" I asked. "Is this another cruel joke?"

His face grew sad as mine grew angry.

"I hoped you would understand. I was only trying to live. That's why you are human, why you are you today."

His words filled me with disgust, saying that I should understand.

"What did you think would happen? What did you think was enough? First my soul, and then my heart. You've destroyed everything that makes me human."

"The point was only to show you what life is really like. That people can be happy together. It wasn't meant as a joke."

What is He doing? Telling me His intentions? Coming from God, I fell into rage.

"Would you dare to tell me that you didn't know what would happen? That everything you've ever done has only ever caused me suffering?"

"I had to give you a choice. What else makes life worth living? All I can do is let you choose. But first I must make you see the choices."

"Are you blaming me? For everything that you've done? Are you blaming me, saying it's *my* fault? *I* made the wrong choices?" I was crying. A sad and bitter rage.

"Yes," He said, "it is. You did." His voice was soft and gentle. Pained with tangible guilt. "But that is just the point: now you know what was wrong. Now you know what makes you human and everyone all the same."

I had enough. God. Lecturing me. About what it means to be human. So I let it all out.

"Do you even know the world you've created? Do you even know anybody in it? They think they know you. I thought I knew you. We beg you to help us. We beg you to fix us. But you're the one who makes us, and you're the one who breaks us. Everything that's

175

gone wrong, you could have made right. Every tear I've ever shed was drawn by your hands."

Then I watched as God changed form. His shape shifted from face to face. All the people I ever knew. And everyone I didn't. Person after person, a countless number. Until finally He stopped. He disappeared. No longer in the mirror. Now standing right beside me. There He was: He become She. Her recently-shaved hair. Her gray-blue eyes. The face from my dream.

"Do you know how I feel?" She asked.

I was feeling every emotion. All my sadness. All my anger. All my pain. And the feeling that I felt, knowing this stranger. The person that I met, the realization of my dream. The heartbreak I felt when she went after we only just had met.

And I wanted to say that I knew. That Her heart was filled with contempt. But I felt it in our connection. I could see it in Her face. That this was the God I knew. And She felt the pain of the entire human race.

"Yes," I said. My lips trembled. "Now I understand."

And just like that, She was gone. I was left alone with my reflection. So I sat at my bed. And I prayed for mercy. I had learned God was dead. As was everybody else.

The Darkness

Do you see the darkness? I hope that you don't. I pray you never do. The darkness is everywhere, but seeing it is a curse. You'd be better off naïve. To not know that it exists. It closes in, all around, consuming everything it can touch. There is not a thing in this world that could be any worse.

Like a disease, it spreads, starting with the heart. First you lose your feelings; you no longer have a spark; there's no more light in your eyes. And that is how it enters: you welcome the dark; then it spreads from your chest, slowly corrupting your mind. Light becomes darkness, smiles become frowns. Purpose is lost, there is none you can find. You lose all your will, you lose all desire. The only things untouched are your darkest of thoughts.

They are what remain when this curse runs its course. You are no longer good enough. You are no longer free. Nobody wants you. Nobody cares. And you did this to yourself, this you can see. The fault is all yours, and you don't know what to do. Every decision you have made has led to this moment. This is on you. You should have known better.

That is when the darkness closes in. After it has left. Because you can see the light. It once made you happy. And now you are not. You don't know if you can be. Or if you ever shall. So when you see others, you are filled with envy. You long for their life, for any at all. So when you see them happy, your face becomes a frown. When you see the light, you wrap yourself in the dark.

It's where you belong. The only place you feel comfort. This is your home because you have made it so. Such is your destiny, the will of this world. To forever have nothing. To be lost and alone. Yet you are young – a shame as it is. You have so much time. If only it were fun.

You'll never belong. You'll never fit in. The only satisfaction you will ever know is constant distraction from the world you let go. Worlds that aren't yours. People you don't know. Places you haven't been. Thoughts you haven't had. There's nothing life can offer – nobody else has it this bad.

And that is your life. In the darkness. You've shut out the light. You've locked the door. You made sure no one can enter – not anymore. And you drown yourself in sorrow, keep digging the hole.

Some people are lucky. It isn't always so bad. They grow tired of the heartache, so they get off the ground. They make their way over and open the door. First, they're blinded by the light – though the sun hasn't risen. Other people see them, and that fills them with fear. But they overcome the temptation to turn back and disappear. So they carry on into the night. Walking in the darkness. Curious to see this new world they have made.

But life is shared with others, so what are they to do – when somebody else asks them how they're doing? "All is well," they say to all who ask. "Now go away," they say to all their friends and anyone from their past. "I can manage on my own," they tell themselves. "I don't need anybody else," they quickly become convinced.

I hope you don't know what it is that I'm saying. Let your confusion be a sign that you are still alive. Because those who see the darkness can never unknow. Every person they see carries two shadows in tow. Every touch they feel is the blade of a knife. Every word they hear is an insult in mind. Every smile they see is a deceitful mask. Every helping hand is given out in pity. Every joy felt is a new depth they must fall.

Be mindful of your shadow. Don't let it wander free. Shine a light, if you can, if it isn't too late. Because darkness is closing. It comes for us all. If you look for it, you'll find it. Then it will find you. You'll know what you are seeing. When it is too late. There's nothing you can do. It consumes the whole world. Starting with your mind.

You become the void. You feed off of others. You take away their joy. You leave them in darkness. By being yourself, you trap others inside. The darkness is you, and you are who spreads it. Where a person once was is now just a hole. Be careful of others lest they trip in the dark. Lest you be responsible for killing their spark.

The light ends with you. None makes it past. The weight of the world sits on your shoulders. Because you are the only one who sees that the world is you. If anything is to be gained from knowing the darkness, it is that this is the only thing which is ever true: you are responsible; this is your world. You did this to yourself, now your heart has gone cold. The sun cannot reach you. You know no more warmth. So what shall you do? You carry the world.

Don't let it fall. Don't let yourself stumble. Make no mistakes and never grow tired. Lest you be the one who makes the world crumble. But where are your friends? Those who could help? Had you not pushed them away, you could finally rest. And those who shine bright cannot see you in the shadow.

How did you get here? What choices did you make? Where do you go? How do you escape? The questions you ask are the only way out. Seeing the darkness should make you angry. Are you not human? Are we not the same? Because others are happy. Yet others feel pain. There's one common factor: that we are ourselves. And our self is human. Why suffer alone? Do you think you have sinned? That you must now atone?

You don't deserve to be forgiven. You don't deserve to be normal. Until you see the darkness for its pitiful lie. That its shadows were cast over your mind. That it's possible to live before you die. No one placed the world in your hands. But you're too distracted to see that you're surrounded by others. Others surround you with worlds of their own. If only you had known that yours could combine. The world is carried by everyone in it. You bore no weight until you went out alone. You brought your world with you – the world and its shadow.

Such is the darkness hidden all around. That those hiding in the shade hide all alone. And those who shine brightest have always known. They cannot see you, but you can see them. You watch them with envy, but they know the darkness. They know what it's like. They saw themselves – that they were the world. The darkness gave them power. It made them aware. Though the cost was great, they took action – gained newfound perspective. So if you want to be free, all you must do is step out. If you want to be seen, just ask them for help.

I went for a walk today, down by the pond
I met a strange man, and of me he seemed rather fond

I tried to speak with him, but all he could do was stare

I looked around
He made no sound
His expression grew afraid

I stepped closer
He stepped closer
Until we stood face to face

His mouth would move but made no sound
"Perhaps you'd feel better on solid ground"

His eyes lit up
He seemed to know:
Into the water, I should go

And though I could not see nor hear
I knew that he overcame his fear

The water was too cold for me
But I knew my actions had set him free

That strange man
Surely now, he'd gone to land

About the Author

Jonathan Swerdlow grew up in an international community where he was exposed to individuals from all worldly backgrounds. Additionally, he spent most of his life traveling the world, engaging in eclectic activities including sailing to Antarctica, studying religion in Tunisia, and accidentally participating in a crystal skull ritual in underground tunnels deep beneath Bosnia.

Jonathan has a formal education in computer science, mathematics, and photography. For most of his life, he worked as an academic researcher, giving talks and lectures in addition to having his work published in peer-reviewed journals. While he still pursues academic endeavors on occasion, Jonathan shifted his focus away from his PhD to pursue creative outlets.

Photography was originally meant as a hobby, but it quickly grew into a love for art, leading Jonathan to spend time living in Europe. During this period, he discovered a passion for writing, starting with poetry – an influence that can be seen in the stories he now writes.

As an artist, Jonathan's motivation is to capture other worlds. As an author, he seeks to create a human world. Utilizing his life experience for perspective, his goal is to move others to see that the meaning of life is other people, and finding meaning in others begins with understanding them. And to understand others, you must first understand yourself. Jonathan hopes to share these beliefs, aid in the process of understanding, and create a more empathetic world through his writing.

Additional work and information can be found at:
www.jonathanswerdlow.com